The Green Leaves of Nottingham

Pat McGrath, a fifth-former in a London comprehensive school, was 14 when he wrote this novel. His amazing gifts of observation have combined with an incredibly mature talent to produce a novel that gives a devastatingly real portrait of a group of young people in an industrial town.

Jamie Howe has returned home after two years in Borstal. No happy homecoming awaits him. His parents do not want him, his friends prefer to forget him, his enemies still bear old grudges. Jamie pals up with Dion Kilgrady, an Irish boy fresh from Borstal himself, and obviously prospering from a highly-organized criminal racket. As Jamie becomes involved with Kilgrady, he finds himself in a situation where robbery leads to blackmail and finally to murder—and where all his attempts at forming lasting human relationships end in disaster.

THE GREEN LEAVES OF NOTTINGHAM

Pat McGrath

Foreword by Alan Sillitoe

W. H. ALLEN   London   1970

Printed in Great Britain
by Northumberland Press Ltd.
Gateshead
for the publishers W. H. Allen & Co. Ltd.
Essex Street, London W.C.2
Bound in Bungay by Richard Clay
(The Chaucer Press) Ltd.
ISBN 0 491 00214 9

FOREWORD

I have never met Pat McGrath but I do know that he writes a good story. Someone told me he was fourteen when he wrote this novel—though only after I'd finished reading it—but I would have written this brief foreword anyway.

I read the book at one sitting. Wild horses couldn't have dragged me from it, because from the first chapter, when Jamie is going back to Nottingham from Borstal, up to the appalling climax in the scrapyard, Pat McGrath handles his material with that panache which is only usually available to a person writing his first novel, or to a novelist who has solved the initial problems of his development.

The Nottingham of this story is of course authentic, and being authentic could be any English industrial city where the poor stay poor because they find it their only final defence against those who say they should not be poor but never give them the means to be otherwise. In English society all trust has broken down. Families are shattered, trade unions are only another part of government repression, radio and television pour out nothing but pompous bilge, social agencies of assistance only exist to break the final vestiges of spirit before stuffing sanctimonious bread into mouths already vomiting back their words. The mass of the people is alienated both from each other and from the more knowing and intelligent strata of society who might be able to help them. But it is too late. The poor of this country are here for ever, running their own sprawling republic of violence and squalor. Nothing is done for them.

Pat McGrath's novel comes straight out of this. It tells a good story, not entirely filled out in parts, but the message underneath rings true enough. The pages burn along at a young man's rate, and if everyone who knew from puzzled and bitter experience what he was talking about, read it, it would be a best seller indeed.

ALAN SILLITOE

Wittersham
January, 1970.

ONE

No buses ever went up Tennon Street, the boy on the train said to himself as he lit a cigarette. Tennon Street is the long, long busy road hidden away by a city ashamed of it. The street will always remain the same and people will always want to hide it from visitors. And yet, the boy thought, it can't be the only street of its kind in the place. Just a busy road like any other. Cars and lorries up it all day making it look like a plain ordinary street. Except that no buses ever ran up or down it. No green buses.

It was a good shopping place. Plenty of shops, a cinema, three pubs, a library and a school. But a bad area. Most of the backstreet men were in prison or had experienced it or soon would experience it. The neighbours would have a good gossip about you as the police van carted you off, but as soon as you were back they'd look down on you as if you were dirt. The children grew through the James Ruffnall School along with the Juvenile Court, Probation Offices, Attention Centres, Detention Centres, Borstal, and on into prison.

No, there's nothing good about Tennon Street because even the leaves that should be on the trees grow somewhere else. There's no green leaves on Tennon Street and all the weeds killed all the flowers in the gardens years ago.

The boy on the train smiled to himself as he thought back on the times he had had on Tennon Street. As a school-

boy. With his friend Bob Denham and, later, Don Gordon.
Don Gordon! Just a few minutes after he had lit the cigarette he was stubbing it out and pressing it into the ash tray.

Get even wi' that Gordon one day, by Christ. And it'll
be soon now. Yes, it would be soon now. The two of them
would be meeting up again that day, or the day after or the
day after that. But sooner or later they'd bump into each
other and it would be then that he, Jamie, would squeeze
the yellow out of that Don Gordon, like a spot.

Jamie looked out of the window as the train entered
Nottingham Midland Station. He looked down at the dead
crumpled cigarette.

Wonder if they've changed Tennon Street any while I've
been away? he asked himself, then answered: Nah! It never
will. I bet there's still kids runnin' up an' down screamin'
and bawlin' with barking dogs chasing them. The walls'll
still be the same as they were when I left. My wall will be,
anyroad.

His wall was the wall at the back of the car park of the
most popular pub on Tennon Street: The Green Leaves.
Every Friday night him and his mates, after having a go at
the slot machines in a café on New Tennon Street, used to
go to the chip shop and from there to The Green Leaves'
car park and 'Jamie's wall'. Jamie would give them permis-
sion to sit on his wall and they'd sit up there eating chips
and watching to see how many couples under eighteen
they knew would go inside.

'I remember when they knocked the old wall down to
build my wall,' Jamie had often announced. 'It 'ad 'ardly
bin up two days before it 'ad more writin' scratched on it
than the old un ever 'ad in twenty years.'

They all remembered.

Tennon Street—
Thugs seek
Windows to break
And girls to rape.
There's no escape.

'Who's the poet?' Jamie had asked Bob Denham and Lynn, the teenage girl who knocked about with the gang, one Friday evening when he discovered it. They didn't know and Jamie grinned. 'Isn't that typical of some Tennon-Streeter?'

Jamie still felt that he had been pushed about for too long. By his parents, teachers, prefects, coppers, probation officers and masters. Two years away from Tennon Street had taught him a lot. And now he was returning to show them all what exactly it was that he had been taught.

'Not much more'n a boy when they put me in Kellowyn,' he'd say to them, and it would make him feel real big. 'But that place 'as toughened me up. I'm no kid now and I'm gonna show 'em that an' all. The Old Man, Gordon, Curris —the lot of 'em.'

The train had stopped and the boy swung himself round the doorway and out on to the platform with his suitcase in his hand. The platform was full of people. People meeting people but nobody to meet him because it was understood by everyone at home that he would not be returning to Tennon Street. Indeed he had made it clear before the police came for him that he'd never go back to Nottingham again.

Jamie started up the steps to the ticket collector following the crowd. Yes, there had been a time when Jamie had been nothing like a toughie. The day he walked into the high school in short trousers and white ankle socks. A victim for the jokers and the bullies. When his mother had

9

told his father about the bigger kids getting on to Jamie at school, Wilf had shrugged his shoulders and said, 'He'll just 'ave ter fend for 'issen.' Jamie and his father had never really got on together anyway.

Jamie came through the booking hall, past the bookstall, past the taxi rank and down the road towards the city centre. He'd go and have a look round there first. The shopping centre was thick with the Saturday crowd. He stopped at Woolworths and decided he'd have a traipse round, then he'd go on to Slab Square, and slowly make his way back towards home.

New Tennon Street leads off of Housenal Street and runs down in to Tennon Street. There are many shops on New Tennon as well. Tennon Street runs downwards into a slummy-looking part at the Lower Rain Street end—houses with rooms to let owned by middle-aged men and women who made a point of knowing everybody's business but their own.

Down the old familiar backstreets Jamie now came, eating grapes, his suitcase under his arm. Still the old dump it always was, he said to himself, spitting out the pips. Still, it's only been two years. Two years ain't really that long. But they've been a lifetime to me.

'Jamie 'Owe!' shouted a female voice from behind. 'Jamie Howe! Warrere yo' doin' back?'

Jamie turned round. It was Sheila, a girl who had been in his class at school. 'Heyup kidder,' he grinned.

'What are yer doin' back?' she repeated. She was a plain-looking girl, dressed in a stained pink blouse, scruffy grey skirt and black stockings. Already the image of her mother, Jamie thought.

'Christ, I only got two years, yer daft cow, not life.' Jamie popped another grape into his mouth. 'I didn't kill anybody, or owt, did I?'

'I wouldn't purrit past yer,' she said. 'I just never thought we'd see you back here again—after all you said about Tennon Street. Come back ter mek trouble, ey yer?'

'Are yer daft, love?' Jamie grinned. 'Anyroad, don't tell anybody you've seen me will yer?'

'Why?' asked Sheila, sitting on somebody's garden wall. 'Escaped or summat?'

'You know better un that,' said Jamie. 'Just don't talk. See you about.'

He went on and in a few minutes Jamie was looking down Tennon Street. It still looked bleak and miserable. Jamie reminded himself that there was nothing, and never had been anything sweet about his home. Nothing sweet about the place or the people who had surrounded him since his birth.

Jamie walked down to the second turning to the right leading off of Tennon Street. This was Deighton Street where he lived. He walked along looking at the windows to see if any of the Pinnocchio-nosed gossips were watching him. None seemed to be. Yet he guessed that as soon as he had passed they'd all be hanging over each other's garden gates.

He stopped at a bright yellow gate with the number 54 on.

So the old man's painted it all up, he smiled to himself as he pushed the gate open. He walked up the three steps to the black and yellow door and hammered on it with the door-knocker. The door-knocker was quite new. It hadn't been there when he was last around.

Nobody answered and after a few minutes he bent down and peeped through the letter-box. He yelled, 'Mam! Mam! Heyup, our Mam, are yer there?'

No answer. He knocked again.

'Come on. Open up. It's me, Jamie! What's up? That ole

sod got you locked up in the cupboard or summat?' When nobody answered that, he whistled for his dog.

'Calamity! Come on duck. Come on Calam! 'ere, girl. Cats! Cats!'

He stood up straight and leaving his case on the top step, went round to the back garden. He knocked on the back door but nobody came. So he returned to his case on the top step at the front door. Now what? How long will I have to wait? he asked himself.

The door-knocker had a lion's head on it. He took a closer look. His old man had a mate who made them and Jamie knew that somewhere there would be a hiding place for the key. He lifted the knocker and examined it carefully. He pushed and pulled in several places, then stuck his thumb under the chin of the lion. The brass face came up, revealing the key hanging on a hook inside the head. Clever, Jamie smiled, pleased with himself for finding it. He unlocked the door, replaced the key in its hiding place, carried his case inside and closed the front door behind him.

The passage had been done up with bright wallpaper. Different from the old, dark stuff that used to make the passage so grim.

'Mam!' Jamie called. 'Calamity, girl!' But the house remained silent.

Jamie carried his case into the living room. Here the furniture had been moved about and there were some new chairs. The cuckoo clock on the wall was gone and a new chromium one replaced it. He put his case on the floor and picked up a piece of paper from the table. It was a note, reading:

Wilf. Gone shopping. Dinner is cooking on slow heat. Dot.

Jamie screwed up the note and left it on the table. Then

he went into the scullery, turned Wilf's dinner off and brought it back to the living room with a knife and fork that had been left there for Wilf. Jamie sat at the table, and enjoyed Wilf's lamb chops, cabbage and potatoes—the best dinner he'd had for ages. Just think, he told himself, that old slob's bin fillin' 'issen wi' grub like this while I've been eatin' pig crap for two years.

After that he sprawled in one of the new armchairs and lit a fag. He was so warm and comfortable that he fell into a snooze, only waking up to look at the clock occasionally.

An hour later he opened his eyes to the sound of the front door opening and closing. He heard his father's voice.

'Ow am I supposed ter know? I usually drive you downtown so you can do yer shoppin' on Sat'dee *afternoons.*'

'Well, I didn't know you was gonna go off ter the pub, did I?' asked the old lady. 'It's your fault if your dinner's burnt ter nowt, an' it will o' done by now, an' all.'

The living-room door opened and his parents stood there, staring. For a few long moments there was a strange silence.

Jamie smiled. 'Heyup Mam! Dad!'

'Jamie!' gasped Dot. 'You're back!.'

'Ah!' said Wilf. 'An' I'd like ter know why. I thought we'd come to an agreement before you came out o' that place.' Wilf closed the door behind him.

'Ah'll tell yer like it is, Dad,' said Jamie. 'I a'n't got a place in 'ell or anywhere to go. No digs or owt.'

'I don't care,' shouted Wilf, 'I told you when we com' to see yer in Borstal! I told you three months ago ter stay away. Might 'ave guessed you'd be back. Well, we don't want owt ter do wi' yer!'

'*Wilf!*' cried his wife.

'Look, I'm gerrin' a job,' Jamie went on. 'I can pay for the room if you're gonna be like that.'

13

'Listen 'ere,' said Wilf, pointing a finger. 'You was the talk of the street after they carted you off. Then the talk died down, and now you're back the neighbours'll be peepin' through their curtain's an' gossipin' over their garden gates again.'

'Oo cares?' cried Jamie. 'Stuff 'em! Lerrem talk. Can't 'urt yer.'

'We got tired of being pointed at, lad,' said Wilf. 'We don't even want you in *Nottingham*, never mind the 'ouse.'

'Stop it, Wilf,' demanded Dot. 'He's got nowhere to go.'

'Well he better gerrout an' start lookin' then,' hollered Wilf. 'I don't wan' 'im 'ere, an' we ain't *'avin'* the cocky little cuss here. So pick up your bag an' start makin' tracks.'

'Wilfred—'

'I'm gerrin' me dinner now,' said Wilf. 'An' if he ain't gone be the time I come back in here wi' it, there'll be trouble.'

'He's stoppin',' said Dot firmly.

'You stop stickin' up for him Dot!' Wilf ordered. 'Made him into a right mam's lad, a'n't yer? I wonder how he's been feelin' in Kellowyn wi'out his mammy all the time. It was the same when he was at school. You stopped him doin' 'omework because you said it kep' him up too late. That was because he never started doin' his homework till the film on telly finished.'

'Look, mek up your minds about whether I'm stayin' or not,' said Jamie, impatiently. ''Cos I've got a lot to do and I'm wastin' an *'ell* of a lot of time sittin' 'ere listenin' to you two scrappin'.'

'I've told yer to get up and clear off, 'aven't I?'

'Wilf, he's your son,' moaned Dot. 'You can't turn him out.'

'He stopped bein' my son when he was thirteen,' snapped Wilf. 'The sticky-fingered lirrle monkey coul'n't keep his

14

hands off owt. Nowt was safe wi' our Jamie around at the market. We 'ad nothin' but police courts, probation officers, the lot. 'E wa' never out o' trouble.'

'Christ, I was a kid then,' argued Jamie, irritably. 'I thought it was in all kids to knock things off an' cut up rough sometimes. It's just that I saw a lot of other kids wi' nice things an' yo' never gen me owt special that was nice, so it 'appened from that. I've changed since then, Da'. Honest to God. I mean, a couple of years in a place like where I've just come from changes a bloke, by Christ it does! It's 'ard. I hated it. Couldn't gerrout quick enough . . . *and* I'm not goin' back. Yeh, it was just big thrills for me—stealin'.'

'Among other things,' said Wilf, raising his eyebrows.

'Look, Dad,' snapped Jamie, anger creeping into his voice. 'I'm tellin' yer I never touched that Valerie and I'll tell yer summat else. I wouldn't touch that lyin' tart wi' a vaultin' pole. An' that Gordon's a lyin' bogger an' all.'

'Yo' an' 'im an' Denham are three of a kind,' said Wilf.

'Look I'll pay owt reasonable to kip 'ere,' said Jamie. 'Nowhere else to go.'

'Let 'im, Wilf,' said Dot.

'Got any money?' Wilf wanted to know.

'Hm,' said Jamie. 'Curris gen me some before I come out. He's a two-faced bleeder. Nice as pie he was as I was leaving to "take my place in society as a respectable citizen", or whatever the prat was ramblin' on about. I was too busy thinking about gettin' outside to listen or care about what he was sayin'. Yeh, nice as pie 'e was. Five minutes before he'd been shoutin' an' bawlin' like some stewed up sergeant-major. Got me a job local, 'e 'as, wi' Knight and Drew's in Hadley Yard—though I'd rather not tek owt off him. Except that sneaky grin on his ug-mug. But I suppose I'll have to tek the job. Especially now I've got to pay rent like a lodger to live in my own home until I'm twenty-one.'

'You bet you'll have to pay like a lodger,' said Wilf. 'And I haven't said you can stay yet.'

'Come on, our Wilf, let him,' pleaded Dot.

Wilf was silent for a few minutes. Then, 'Yer. Hm, all right . . .'

Jamie was amazed. 'Wha'?'

'You can stay,' said Wilf. He gave a Curris-styled grin. 'As long as you lay three quid on that table every Fridee night.'

'Are you daft, Dad?' cried Jamie. 'I could rent a furnished room for that or get digs or summat.'

'Do that then, I couldn' care less,' said Wilf, sharply. 'It's either three quid a week or get out now. I don't mind. We could do wi' the money but we ain't so desperate that we couldn't goo wi'out it. There's ter be rules an' all but I'll give them a bit of thought. Well. Tek it or leave it.'

Jamie sighed. He leaned forward and opened his suitcase. He took out two half-pint bottles of brown ale. 'Dropped by the beer-off. Got a couple o' bottles in. Thought we might celebrate my 'ome-comin', like. I a'n't 'ad none o' this stuff since I whipped that bottle at Aunt Glad's Christmas party, once. D'yer remember?'

'Out of Borstal five minutes an' he's spendin' his money away on ale,' declared Wilf.

'Ey, come on, Dad,' grinned Jamie. 'Yo've supped some ale in your time, an' all, a'n't yer?'

Wilf grunted and left the room. Jamie got up, looked around him and found a bottle-opener and a white cup. He took the top off one of the bottles and poured his mother a drink in the cup.

Dot was a small woman who looked older than she really was—probably because she never wore make-up or smart clothes, and because her thick stockings were always

16

crumpled round her ankles. Her hair was untidy and beginning to go grey. Yet she looked happier than Wilf.

'I'm glad you're back, Jamie,' she smiled. 'I'd bin workin' on your father, honest. But I want you to promise me this. You'll keep your 'ands to yersen, won't yer? I don't want to see 'em cart you back off to that place again.'

'Don't worry, Mam,' Jamie smiled. 'It was only a lark wi' me an' Don. An', I di'n't touch that Valerie. She's a liar.'

He gave her the half-filled cup, then finished off the rest out of the bottle himself.

'Where's Calamity, Mam?'

'Oh, Jamie—didn't yer know?'

'Know what? How could I know anything when you only came to see me once and I never got so much as a letter! What's 'appened?'

Dot looked uncomfortable.

'She's buried in the garden,' she said. 'I'd just got 'er a licence and yer Dad wa' so mad 'e took 'er in the garden wi' 'is air rifle an' . . .'

But before Jamie could express his anger and horror, Wilf stormed back into the room. 'Thought you 'ad me dinner on!'

'I did,' said Dot. 'What's 'appened? Burnt away to dust, 'as it?'

'It ain't there at all, woman!' Wilf bellowed. His eyes turned to Jamie, now fumbling, trying to open the second bottle. Wilf looked from him to the empty plate on the table and then back to Jamie again. 'You greedy bogger!'

'*Well*—I was 'ungry,' Jamie shouted back. 'An' anyway, what about my do—?' But Wilf didn't let him finish. He bellowed again, 'In 'ere two minutes and you're scoffin' my bleedin' dinner. And wi' no idea that I'm gonna allow you to stay here either.'

'I'll cook yer summat else, Wilf,' pleaded Dot, but Wilf turned on her.

'Yer can keep yer cookin' for 'im. I'm goin' back up the pub.' He slammed out of the front door and they heard the clang of the garden gate.

Jamie gave a deep sigh.

'Huh, welcome 'ome. Tuh!'

TWO

Don Gordon was cleaning a motor bike outside 28 Deighton Street when Jamie came out of his house later that day. He was squatting in the road, working hard with a piece of rag, a tin of polish beside him on the pavement. Don didn't see Jamie walk towards him, but he suddenly became aware of someone standing over him, watching.

'Well, well, well,' said Jamie. 'If it ain't the local child-problem 'issen, in person. Don Gordon . . . with the per-sonal-psychological-problem. Tell me. D'yer still sit cryin' in public places like you used to do when you wa' sixteen?'

Don looked up slowly.

'Jesus, *you're* back!' Then he looked down again and carried on with what he was doing. 'Welcome 'ome.'

Jamie came nearer the bike. 'Warrare yo' doin' up 'ere? You live down the lower end.'

'Not now I don't,' said Don. 'I live 'ere. 28. With a mate o' mine from London.'

'Left your old lady on 'er jack, ey yer?'

'Mm.'

'Not yourn is it?' Jamie asked, patting the seat of the bike.

''Arf of it is. My mate gorrit, an' I'm payin' 'arf.'

'Nicked some more money?'

Don stood up and dropped the piece of rag on the seat of the bike. He looked quickly at Jamie then back to the bike.

'Now listen ter me. I proved it two years ago that I 'ad nowt ter do wi' that forty-eight quid, an' I can prove it. Now I don't need to prove it to you because you bloody well know it. It wa'n't a very strong story yer gave the scuffs, but then yo' 'ad ter think fast, didn't yer!'

Jamie threw his arms out and grabbed Don by the neck of his pullover. He dragged him as close as he could but the motor bike was between them.

'Don't gimme that bull, Gordon,' Jamie snarled. 'Yo' 'ad me cop for summat I didn't do because yer wa' yeller. Well watch your bloody step, Gordon, cos one o' these dark nights you'll find my fist flying in your face—and worse.'

'It can work both ways,' said Don.

Jamie fastened his grip on Don's pullover. 'You've 'ad it! I'll get even wi' you an' I'll see the right one of us gets put away this time.' He let go and pushed Don away. 'So long, kidder. I'll be seein' yer.'

'I'll look forward to that,' said Don. Jamie moved on and Don watched him until he was a good way up the street. Then he bent down, put the lid on the polish tin and went into the house.

Don shared the basement with a boy called Tommy Bryan. Tommy was twenty, but looked younger, blond, small, but thick-set. Don had met him around Tennon Street a few weeks before, just after he'd arrived from London. He knew Tommy had been working as some kind of salesman, but now he hadn't a job; he was going to look for one, he said. Tommy was at the sink having a wash. He hadn't been up out of bed for more than ten minutes.

'Watch'a, Don,' he grinned, picking up a towel and drying himself. 'What's up? You look like yer've seen a ghost or somethin'.'

'I 'ave. Only this one lives up the road. I 'ate 'is guts and

20

'e 'ates mine. Said 'e were never coming back 'ere again.'

'Oh, he's been away, 'as 'e?' said Tommy, tucking his shirt into his trousers. 'Got somethin' on yer?'

'No! Course 'e 'asn't.'

'Then stop lookin' like a zombie with a problem an' come out an' get some tea.'

They went into the street and Don started towards the motor bike but Tommy stopped him. 'No, not on that. Let's walk. I wanna get an evenin' paper.'

They called in to a newsagents on Tennon Street and then walked round to the café on New Tennon Street. Tommy went to the counter and ordered egg, bacon and chips twice, with two cups of tea. Then the two of them found a table and sat down. Tommy opened his paper at the sports pages.

A few minutes later a group of teenagers came in. One was Sheila, the girl who had spoken to Jamie that morning. They sat at the next table and Sheila said, 'Heyup, Don. 'Ow are yer?'

'Fine,' Don grunted.

'Yer'll not be for long,' chuckled one of the boys, Trev Baldin.

Tommy looked up from his paper.

'Jamie 'Owe's back,' said Sheila.

'Could 'a told yer that mesen,' said Don. 'I've bin talkin' to 'im.'

'You won't be doin' much talkin' to 'im next time you meet,' said Trev. 'Especially now you've practically moved right into Jamie's back yard.' The group of teenagers laughed.

'This the ghost you was talkin' about, Don?' Tommy asked.

'Yeh.'

'Jamie's the lad Don Gordon railroaded, like they say,' said Trev Baldin loudly. 'Gorrim two years-worth o' Borstal. For doin' nowt.'

Tommy looked from Trev to Don. 'S'truth!'

'No,' said Don quickly. 'He got purraway for thievin' forty-eight nicker. He was the only one oo could 'ave whipped it 'cause I didn't. He knows it. He likes people to think he's 'ard-done-by.'

'Jamie 'Owe tells a pretty convincing story, that's all I can say,' said Sheila. ''E'll be after you, so I should watch mesen if I war' yo'.'

One of the teenage boys got up and went to the juke box. He put a record on and the café was filled with sound. A waitress brought a tray carrying the food and Don started eating. Tommy folded his newspaper and put it on the table.

'Tell me about it,' he said.

'About what?' said Don.

'Jamie 'Owe.'

'Oh, not now,' said Don.

'Why not now? I wanna know *now*,' said Tommy.

'I'm eatin' me tea,' protested Don. 'Later! I'll tell yer.'

'Okay. All right,' said Tommy. He started eating, too. They didn't say anything for a few minutes.

Then Don said, 'Juke box music! Guz right through yer, don' it!'

'Don't yer like good music, Don?'

'No, not when I'm tryin' to think.'

THREE

That Saturday evening Jamie stood facing shiny bottles and mirrors in a pub he knew his father wouldn't turn up in. There was hardly anyone else in the bar, and he was talking to Tom, the barman.

'Why did you come back 'ere then, Jamie?' asked Tom, wiping the counter between them. 'You said you'd never come back.'

'Oh, dunno. Bein' in Kellowyn makes you change your mind about a lot of things. I suppose it's easiest comin' back to the place yer know—where yer 'ome's s'pposed to be. Even a dump like this. Besides—they got me this job in Hadley Yard—startin' on Mondee.'

'What did yer old man say?'

''E said "Git out", but 'e changed 'is mind when I said I 'ad money.'

'Word's got about that you're back, a'n' it?' said Tom.

'Yeh. Word's going around, biting every gossiper's backside. There's too many gossipers in our area and it's no wonder there's so many boys and girls in Borstal and men in prison. Nasty rumours an' lies fly around Tennon Street stingin' everybody like soddin' bumble bees. I know summat. I'd never want to get lodgin's around 'ere. Not wi' a landlady that's got a mouth-'ole like a Victorian fireplace.' Jamie paused. 'Not that any of 'em 'ud 'ave me,' he added.

'What wor it like in Kellowyn?' Tom asked. 'I 'ad a

23

nephew there once. Didn't 'ear much from 'im.'

'Depends what yer in for, an 'oo yer get. There was only a few people in Kellowyn that I liked. I hated most of 'em, I can tell you. Not all the masters were bad, but some were rotten sods. Especially the top bloke, Curris. My Christ, there was a bleedin' psycho. He wouldn't o' pushed me an' the lads around if he 'adn't got his staff and his dogs and the rest o' the world to protect him. The world who'd look down on us in Kello' if we had rebelled, and the people what make the world go round, would have said, "Bunch of young ruffians. Couple of years in the Army would do 'em good", when it ud do the bleddy opposite. It'd show us how to kill somebody the easy way so that as soon as we marched from the battlefields where we're fightin', we can come 'ome and kill the people who sent us out there to be killed.

'Curris'ud be the first to gerrit on my list. Cos he'd clout you round the ear'ole any time. Do owt out of place and you were in for it. Most of the lads was scared of him but I tried not to be. You're yourself and no other man can work you like a glove puppet. And I'll tell you who told me that —an Irish bloke called Kilgrady. All the lads liked him because he was a great bloke. My age, or just over, he must have bin. Black 'air an' blue eyes like I never seen blue before. 'E lived in Long Eaton. The lads called him "Irish Reb" 'cos he wouldn't conform wi' the Borstal system. Cheeked the masters off a treat. It got him bashed up by masters loads of times. When they put the shine of their boots in your guts you certainly wished you wa' dead but if you wanted to be respected by the lads—and the masters for that matter—like Kilgrady was, then you didn't break down and give up to them. Not if you wanted to be like Irish Reb.

'He just wouldn't stop givin' them good excuse ter smack

24

him up. Me an' 'im were great mates until he got out a year after I got in and came back up 'ere. When 'e'd gone all the lads laughed at me and said, "Where will you be wi'out Paddy, now, kid? Who's gonner look after you now, eh? Got ter face Grandad Curris all on your lonesome now a'n't yer!" Well I did and that got me a few wallopings an' all. It took me a year to really get me hair up at these masters pushing us around. One of 'em called Armas nudged me in the dining hall one day—accident, admitted—but it knocked my dinner out of my hand and the plate clattered on the floor. He told me I was a daft cat—as if it 'ad been bleddy me who'd done it—and if I didn't clear up the mess I'd be in trouble. Thanks to 'im all that was left of me dinner was the pud, so I got so mad I coughed up a greeny and made his bald head shine. Armas went crax. All the lads laughed and I wished to 'ell Irish Reb 'ad bin there to see it. Armas 'ad me marching down to Curris. I thought I was going to get a dig in the gob and a night in a windowless room, on a bench. But no. I got an 'ell of a caning and whoever said breaking up is 'ard to do was a liar.

'It was me who took over as leader of Irish Reb's little gang. We all made lousy jobs of any stealing we did and a few months before I came out Curris got me in to his study and worked me over like he'd done to Irish Reb and others before.

'"No use tryin' to fight 'em," an experienced lad from Loughborough told me. "You can't win, so you're wastin' your energy tryin".' That didn't stop me getting me hair up and pokin' Curris back in the mush once. He grabbed me and stared into my eyes, sweat running' down his face as he got madder an' madder. He growled between his green teeth, "Think you're a little rebel don't you, Howe? You want to be remembered as a rebel, like Kilgrady, don't you Howe?"

I simply replied, "There's no rebel in me, Sir, just a lot of hate." He said we was all the same. Scruffy little kids taken off of slummy backstreets—which was where I stopped him. I told him our part of Tennon Street wasn't as bad as some parts of Nottingham. Kellowyn was the only slum I'd ever lived in.'

Tom had raised his eyebrows in disbelief at some of Jamie's story.

'So you asked for trouble an' you got it,' he said. 'My nephew didn't think Curris was that bad.'

'Your nephew must be a good-looking lad,' mumbled Jamie.

Tom turned away to serve another customer. Jamie looked down into his half-empty mug. He didn't notice a slim, smartly-dressed boy come in and stand at the counter a few feet away from him. He was a good-looking young man with clear blue eyes and black wavy hair. His suit was grey and well cut. It looked expensive. Flashy cufflinks in gold matched a big ring and tiepin. His shirt was a cream colour and when he spoke he spoke with an Irish accent.

'Hey, chief,' he called to Tom. 'Bring a bottle of whiskey over this end will yer?'

Jamie looked up with a start. He stared in amazement. Then he exploded, 'Bloody 'ell fire! Irish Reb, for Christ's sake!'

The young man looked round. He seemed puzzled for a moment, then he raised a finger. 'Don't I remember you from some place? Ah, sure let me t'ink now . . . Kellowyn Court? Yeh, yeh, that's right. Howe from Tonnon Street. Jim Howe, am I right?'

'Jamie Howe,' smiled Jamie, moving up closer. 'An' it's Tennon Street. Heyup mate.'

'When did you get out?' asked Kilgrady.

26

'Yesterday,' said Jamie. 'On me way from Kellowyn I stopped over at Tommy Drummer's in Leicester until early this mornin'. Then he got a train for the swingin' capital, and I got the train headin' the opposite way and here I am.'

Kilgrady smiled. 'I remember when you first came into Kello'. The governor tellin' you to get that chip off your shoulder, and you sayin' "I would if I had a bloody fork".'

'An' it was Standard who heard me, not Curris,' said Jamie. 'Standard didn't do owt, either. He just told me I'd better tread carefully, because he said he'd be on the alert every time he'd hear my clod-hoppers soundin' down the corridors.'

Tom brought a bottle of whiskey with a glass and set it down in front of Kilgrady. Kilgrady pulled a five-pound note from his wallet.

'What are you drinkin'?'

'Me? Oh, brown. It's okay. I'll buy it.'

'No, no,' Kilgrady insisted. 'I'm buyin'.'

An old man standing near them grunted. 'That's the only good thing about the Irish. Allus willin' ter buy their round. It's the bleedin' Scotch I don't like.'

Jamie grinned at Kilgrady. 'Must have met up wi' a kilt that talked and drank too fast for him!'

Tom brought Jamie another brown ale and then went on to serve somebody else. Jamie thought Tom must realize this was the Irish boy they'd just been talking about.

'Whiskey?' said Jamie, as he watched Kilgrady fill his glass. 'Strong i'n't it?'

Kilgrady sighed. 'My Old Man was a divil for the drink. Known all over Long Eaton for it. And when he was as drunk as drunk could be, widout passing out, he'd grab me and try to pour whiskey down me t'roat. I was about fifteen and I hated the taste of it. Jaysus, it burnt the gut off me and I couldn't stand it until I got out of Kellowyn. Then I got a liking for the old man's killer. T'ank the Mother of Jaysus the old man's dead now. It was because of him I first got landed in Kellowyn. It was me who had to steal his whiskey.'

The bar had filled up now, and Tom was too busy to be able to listen to their conversation.

'What'll you be doin' now you're out?' Kilgrady asked.

'Factory wo'k,' Jamie grunted. 'Curris got me hooked up wi' this firm on Hadley Yard. I start Mondee. Five-minute walk from our street—down the slummy end of Tennon Street. I never fancied factory wo'k. Doin' the same thing over and over again five thousand times a day. I wouldn't be able to stick life in an office either. I'd suffocate while I'd be going mad. I thought quite a bit about careers at school. Somehow I guessed I'd never make owt in life and the effort to try seemed too much of a struggle, so I didn't bother to try. I had ideas like everybody else, but that's life. You *dream* about careers, but in real life—away from your imagination and dreams' reach—you end up sloggin' your guts out in a factory.'

The old man next to them rapped his glass down on the counter, spilling his beer into a large pool.

'That's scratched on every wall of Tennon Street,' he said.

'It wa' me who scratched it there,' grunted Jamie.

'There's always summat for a chap that'll work for it,' the old man went on. 'Trouble wi' yo' is that you can't be bothered ter gerrout an' do a damn good day's wo'k.'

'Stop slobberin' before I'm sick,' moaned Jamie. The old idiot's so drunk he doesn't even know he's talking, never mind what he's talking about, he thought.

Jamie turned back to Kilgrady. He pictured in his mind two Borstal house captains dragging the bloody figure of the

Irish boy who had been beaten up, his lips purple, his eyelids swelling up, blood trickling from his nose to his lips. It had been the last time he had seen Dion Kilgrady—a year ago. He had looked like a victim from the St. Valentine's Day Massacre. Who had attacked him? Had it been a rival rebel? Jamie liked to think it had been Curris.

But now look at Kilgrady. Immaculate. He must be on to something good to roll about dressed like that, Jamie thought.

Kilgrady suggested they take their drinks to a table. So they moved across the room and sat down.

'Bet you're glad to be out aren't you?' smiled Kilgrady.

'Ah, not 'arf,' said Jamie.

'Two years for what?' Kilgrady wanted to know.

'Whippin' forty-eight quid, stickin' up a one-arm bandit and taking advantage of a defenceless girl,' said Jamie. 'Innocent on two accounts. An' all that thanks to a spaz called Gordon and a bitch named Valerie Harpe. Val Harpe! If I had my way she'd be playin' her's now. Her old man owns Harpe's Enterprizes. Me an' my mates used to 'ang about a caf' on New Tennon Street that 'ad one-arm bandits an' things. We'd bust 'em an' collect miniature fortunes. Then we'd go round the fish and chip shop and get two bobs'-worth of fish and chips and a bottle of pop. Well this girl caught us at it once. Nice lookin' bird, too. Smart. You could tell she wasn't a Tennon Streeter. Then me, Don Gordon an' 'er got right pally and we even cut her in. One day we went round her 'ouse. Her old lady had died a couple of years before and Daddy was out. She got the records and the player out, put some on and pulled the curtains. I gave Don Gordon the signal to get lost because I thought "Heyup, yer on to a good thing 'ere". He went. He left me an' Val alone with the record player and the sofa. After all this

29

curtain-pullin' lark and sexy smiles, she dodged every move I made except I did manage to kiss 'er. Then I twigged it had all been a game so I went 'ome.

'Next thing I know the cops are around our 'ouse askin' questions and practically accusin' me of theft and assault. Val's old man had left forty-eight quid lyin' around, the silly sod. An' after me an' Gordon left, so did the forty-eight nicker. When the cops went home for tea I went out and told Don. He laughed and said: "So while yo' was havin' it off wi' 'er they got burglars in the middle of the afternoon, eh?" Seducing her? What, me? I should o' bin so lucky.

'Anyroad, Don said we should forget it, so him and Val Harpe knocked on my door that night and we popped round the caf'. We went sticking up fruit machines and, for the first time ever, we wa' caught by the caf' bloke. While that was 'appenin' the scuffs were back round our house searchin' the place. They found nowt in the 'ouse so they went out to the shed. One scuffer stuck his feeler in my bike's saddle-bag and pulled out forty-eight flaming nicker. I don't have to tell you how it got there, do I? It seems that after I'd told Gordon to drift that afternoon, leavin' me with Valerie, 'e 'adn't done. He'd gone into her old man's bedroom and found that money. Later, when I told him the cops had been around our house asking questions he'd got scared, and before knockin' on our door when him and Val called for me, he'd stuffed the lolly in my saddlebag.

'I knew he'd done it as soon as I saw the copper who came into the room where they'd taken Gordon, Val and me, after we'd got picked up over the fruities. The copper looked at me and said I was in much more serious trouble than for slot machines. When they questioned us, Gordon swore blue murder that he hadn't come back to the house wi' me

30

and Val, that afternoon. Val never said owt good for me either. Just that I'd gone for her wi' a twinkle in me eye. Maybe she and Gordon had thought they'd pinch the money together. Or maybe she was scared when she'd found out the money was gone and she knew it was one of us.

'Anyroad, they couldn't prove that I'd assaulted her. But along we went to the Juvenile Court and Gordon got a year on probation. I was already on probation for being a trouble-making yob before, so I got two years in Kellowyn for the lolly and the fruities. They had me hooked good and proper. Val got off with a warning to keep out of trouble in future.'

Jamie paused and took a gulp of his beer, then added thoughtfully, 'Mind you—if I'd've *known* that the money was there I might have nicked it.'

Kilgrady laughed.

'Are you going to lead a clean, straight life now?' he asked.

'Do you?'

'Sure, I do.'

Jamie laughed. 'Nah! You? That'll be the day! Yo' never went straight.'

'Shows that much?' asked Kilgrady.

'Yeh! It's a wonder you ain't been picked up for questioning by a suspicious scuffer, all ponced up in a suit like that,' said Jamie. 'How much did it rush yer?'

'Forty pounds,' Kilgrady told him proudly, pouring more whiskey from the bottle into the glass.

'Teks my old man two weeks to earn that,' said Jamie. 'And I can't see you in one of them regular well-paid jobs.'

'Sure it's a suspicious mind ye've got there, Jamie,' said Kilgrady. 'And, for Christ's sake, don't you know we never talk about work in a pub?'

'I know why *you* don't,' said Jamie. 'What yer doin', Dee? Carryin' on the tradition of Sherwood Forest?'

'I'm minding my own business and gettin' along fine.'

'How many years would you get if you was caught now?' Jamie went on, undeterred.

'Listen—just because I'm wearin' a very fine suit, drivin' a nice little van and drinkin' what I like, as much as I like, *when* I like, you mustn't start thinkin' things about my manner of business.' Then, unable to resist the boast, he added in a whisper, 'Between fifteen and twenty years I suppose.'

Jamie whistled. 'My Christ! Some business!' he exclaimed softly. 'Can't yer tell me about it?'

Kilgrady rubbed his nose. 'Maybe I could be telling you if you was willin' to earn yourself a suit like this.'

'Very risky?'

'Jaysus, if there was no risks wouldn't everybody be t'ieves an' murderers?' replied Kilgrady.

'Well you'll have to tell me more before I commit mesen,' said Jamie. Kilgrady leaned forward with his elbows on the table.

'I've told you we never talk business in a place like this.'

'Then let's go. Christ it's 'ot! Anyway I don't like this pub.'

'No, I'm stayin' here.'

'Why? You got a van. Let's tek a drive out to the country pubs up Donnington way.'

'I've told you I can't go. I'm waitin' for a girl.'

'Ah, I see. I wondered what you was doin' 'ere. What's this tart's name?'

'She's not a tart and her name's Dolly Benson,' said Kilgrady.

'What's she like? Wear short skirts?'

32

'Short enough.'

'Got long hair?'

'Hm.'

'Blonde?'

'No, dark.'

'Good, I'm glad,' said Jamie. 'Is she Nottinghamish?'

'She's from here, yes.'

'Does she know what you do for a livin'?'

'Yeh.'

'An' she don't mind?' Then Jamie's look of surprise faded. 'I bet she don't. As long as the paper money keeps on floating out of your mitts and into her purse she'll not mind.'

'You've been in Kellowyn too long, Jamie,' said Kilgrady. 'Boys locked up in a place like that, seein' nuttin' but boys —it gives 'em funny attitudes towards girls from then on.'

'Rammel!' said Jamie. ''As Dolly got a friend for me? Anyway, when are you goin' to tell me what you *was* goin' to tell me? About your business?'

'Come outside for some air if it's too hot in here for you,' said Kilgrady, getting up and putting the top on his bottle of whiskey. 'Hey, chief,' he called to Tom, 'mind that till I get back, will yer!' And he pushed the bottle along the counter towards Tom.

They went outside and stood where they could see the door in case Dolly arrived.

'Well,' said Kilgrady, 'me and my partner are up here doing some grand work. I live here in Nottingham with me partner and lately t'ings have been goin' along smoodly. Just like a dream. But we've got to watch what could be a nasty bit of opposition moving in on us, and we might be able to use some help from a bright boy like yerself. But in your spare time, y'understand. Ye'll have to take your job in the factory and then see how you get on with us.'

33

'What's this opposition you're talking about?'

'Adam Clint and two of his tough boys moved in from London 'n' Manchester clubs last week.'

'Adam Clint?' said Jamie. 'Who's 'e?'

'He's got his hands in a lot of enterprises at the moment,' said Kilgrady. 'He's an operator. His uncles in America were killed on the same day as Dillinger and in the same way. When big companies go bankrupt the chances are it's Mr. Clint's doin'. He's a confidence trickster. He takes over businesses that were once good and genuine and swindles the public when they come to him. He'll do anything—forgery, embezzlement, robbery, even murder. He was once a barrow boy on Berwick Street Market in Soho. But he's up in the world now and his interests are spreading. He's a very wealthy man—also a very dangerous one.'

'Where is 'e now?' asked Jamie.

'In the Carnden Hotel, a mile away. I don't know why he's here but I kind of wish he wasn't.'

'You're prob'ly makin' a fart into a thunderstorm,' grinned Jamie. 'I bet he doesn't even know you exist.'

'My partner says he knows Clint,' said Kilgrady.

'What? Friends?'

'Yes.'

'What's there to worry about then?' Jamie asked. 'If he's your mate you're safe.'

'If we're bad for Clint's business, we're not safe,' said Kilgrady.

'Christ, why should a bloke like that want to come here?' asked Jamie.

'Nottingham's growing,' said Kilgrady. 'Maybe Clint has a few ideas about the place.'

'He'd go where the money is,' Jamie assured him, as if he knew all about it. 'And if he's wanted he can't start a club or owt up here can he? Not without licences.'

'He doesn't advertise his name in lights outside his clubs!' exclaimed Kilgrady. 'Sure he owns them, but other people run them for him. Influential people.'

'So you think you could be findin' yoursen in a round of violence?' asked Jamie.

'I'm just on the alert, that's all,' said Kilgrady. 'If ever it comes to bullets flyin', I'm off out of it, probably back home to Ireland. Clint won't have ter tell me twice.'

'I'm interested in joining you and your partner as long as there's no violence,' Jamie said. 'Eight quid a week is all that factory job can offer and I can't see much life in that. But I don't want ter be blasted in different directions across Slab Square.'

'You can come an' meet my partner next Saturday mornin',' said Kilgrady. 'We'll see what he has to say about you comin' in wid us.'

They walked back to the bar again, Kilgrady retrieved his whiskey from Tom and bought Jamie another brown ale. As they sat at a table Jamie realized he had already had more to drink than he was used to. He unbuttoned his shirt at the neck.

Jamie had been awake that Saturday since the early hours, and it had been a long, eventful day. But the beer, the atmosphere and the unaccustomed sensations of new-found freedom had made him tired and after a while he dropped off to sleep with one hand round the bottom of his beer mug.

He felt somebody nudging him. He shook his head, trying to shake off the misty, dream-like atmosphere, and he saw a new face. An attractive teenage girl was sitting at the table between him and Kilgrady. It had been her waking him up.

'Ey too much pop?' she grinned. 'Many more inside you and yer'll be unconscious. You've got an 'ell of a red face. You look right merry.'

'So'd you look right merry if you just came out of Kello' after spendin' two long years in there,' moaned Jamie, trying to sit up.

'Oh, you've been inside too?' said Dolly. 'Another naughty boy.'

'You're an insultin' bitch, aren't you?' said Jamie.

'Don't worry,' said Dolly. 'Me and Dion are criminals too.'

'Bonnie and Clyde,' sneered Jamie. 'I mean: Dion 'n' Dolly or Dolly 'n' Dion who sped about the countryside of Nottinghamshire, England on a tandem shooting the whole countryside up—riddling all the lone scarecrows—and generally raisin' 'ell.'

'Drink up and shut up an' we'll be off,' said Kilgrady, impatiently.

'We're going to take you to meet a friend of ours if ye're a good lad and shut your gob for a while,' said Dolly.

'What friend?' asked Jamie.

'Female,' Kilgrady told him.

'Gerrin' me fixed up wi' a bird?' said Jamie. 'What's she like? Any cop?'

'She's nice,' said Dolly. 'Come on, 'urry up or we'll not tek yer.'

Jamie finished his drink and unsteadily followed Kilgrady and Dolly through the crowd, out of the doors and into the car park. Kilgrady led them to his light blue van and unlocked the doors. Jamie fell in the back and Dolly sat in front beside Kilgrady.

Jamie clung to the side of the van as it started to move. His head swam and his stomach heaved. Kilgrady and Dolly were talking but he didn't try to follow what they were saying.

At last the movement stopped. Kilgrady had parked the van outside a four-storey block of flats. Dolly looked over her shoulder at Jamie. 'Julie's the daughter of a pretty well-off man. Her father's Harold Dean who owns the telly shops. So none of your common talk and vulgar language.'

'Don't you worry about me, boyo,' said Jamie. 'I can pass mesen.'

They got out of the van and Kilgrady locked the doors. Then they went into the flats and up the stairs to the second floor. They stopped at a green door with the letter 'J' on it. Kilgrady rang the bell and soon the door was opened by a girl dressed in grey slacks and a purple sweater. Her blonde hair curled at the shoulders and her bright, pleasant smile greeted them warmly. Blimey! thought Jamie, as he pushed himself off of the wall he was leaning on and stood up straight. He felt suddenly empty inside and thought if he tried to say anything he would mess it up.

'Heyup, Jue,' said Dolly. 'Thought we'd pop round and see if you'd like to nip out for a drink. Mek up a foursome.'

'Come in,' the girl smiled, standing aside. Jamie stepped into a room which looked different from all other rooms he had ever been into.

In one corner was a writing bureau with a lamp next to it that had a red shade. The shade matched red cushions on the white settee which had its back to a wall of green wallpaper. Near the window, where big yellow curtains were drawn, was an armchair that matched the settee. In front of the settee was a coffee table upon which was a portable typewriter and two folders. Standing on the folders was a stem glass of sherry. At the same end of the room as the bureau, only in the other corner, was a television set turned on with the volume low. The carpet was a red wall-to-wall carpet and there was a white rug before the fire-place. An electric fire shot heat across the room and a lamp was on shining down on the typewriter which had a half-typed page in it. A cosy, dimly-lit, smart room, Jamie thought.

The girl closed the door. 'I'd intended writing until about midnight,' she told them.

'Bad night on telly, is it?' Jamie forced himself to ask.

'Pardon?'

'Telly,' said Jamie, feeling uncomfortable and silly. 'Is it a bad night or 'as the sound just gone?'

'Oh, I've only got it on to brighten the room up,' she smiled. 'It looks dull wi'out the telly on at night, and it's more cosy lit up that way.'

'Ah,' said Jamie. He coughed. 'Ah know what yer mean.'

'Julie, this is Jamie—' Dolly turned to Jamie. 'Jamie what?'

'Howe. Jamie Howe, duck.'

'He's already had a bit more than he should've ter drink,' Dolly told Julie. 'He's a bit tipsy, but if you're willin' to take the chance we might ey some fun. Jamie, this is Julie. Julie Dean.'

'Heyup, duck,' smiled Julie.

Jamie looked into her bright blue eyes, got a whiff of the nice smell of perfume about her and felt even more uncomfortably shy. Suddenly he got the feeling he had to do something to impress her. Something to make her like him.

Julie took their coats and Jamie, after uttering a confused 'hello', felt sick as he watched her hang his coat on the hanger. Why the hell hadn't he responded to her greeting like her favourite film star would have done? He felt himself getting redder and redder as sweat began to appear on his

38

face. All of a sudden he was aware of his heart beating. Each beat had a full stop behind it and seemed to have a few seconds' interval before the next. He wasn't used to ale and he wasn't really used to girls—especially girls like this one.

Julie got out glasses and offered them all sherry—apologizing that this was the only drink she had in. Kilgrady said no, so Jamie said no. Dolly accepted.

Jamie sat in the armchair while Dolly and Kilgrady sat on the settee with Julie next to them, behind her typewriter. Dolly told Jamie that Julie had written a book and Julie was quick to add that it had been rejected by eleven publishers and she had given up hope. But Dolly went on to say that *Woman's Play* had accepted one of her short stories called 'J'y suis, j'y reste', which means, she explained, 'Here I am, and here I remain'.

'Congratulations,' smiled Jamie. 'I hope we see yer name in the bestseller lists.'

'Thank you,' she said, 'but I don't suppose you will.'

'Writin' another?' Jamie asked, nodding towards the typewriter.

'Yes,' said Julie. 'It's called "Pour passer le temps", or "In order to pass the time away".'

'Read it to us as far as you've got,' requested Dolly.

'Oh, no!' said Julie, putting the lid back on the typewriter.

'Don't be rotten—read it,' cried Dolly.

'Yeh, goo on,' said Jamie. 'Get readin'.'

After more protests, Julie shrugged her shoulders and began to read the manuscript. After the first five minutes Jamie decided it was too boring to listen to. He'd never read this type of story before. He'd read nothing but crime books all through Kellowyn and before that he'd read war comics

39

and playboy magazines. This romantic dig-dag wasn't his type.

His mind wandered into deep thought. About his family and relations. Most of the relations split up and feuding, scrapping all the time and making Jamie laugh. They had been at it as long as he could remember and he liked to think he was on the outside looking in at them. He didn't want to grow up and be brought into their childish rows because they all looked so damned silly.

The only real good person among his relations was his Uncle Ron. He shared the same opinion of the family as Jamie. Three times Ron had seen the inside of Lincoln Prison, and old Ron hated travelling—especially to and from Lincoln. He always said, 'It's maddenin', our Jamie, it really is. The least the sods could do is put you in Leicester . . .'

'And that's it so far,' said Julie, closing the folder.

Jamie started. 'That's bleddy good,' he said, making sure he got in the first compliment.

'He's right,' Dolly followed.

'He—sure—is,' said Kilgrady, who had been sitting there looking uncomfortable as he fingered a fag that was burning away.

'Thank you very much,' she smiled happily. 'Now I'll go and get changed and come out with you.' She picked up her folders, got up and glided through to the bedroom, closing the door behind her.

'Wow,' hissed Jamie, rubbing his hands together excitedly. 'She's a smasher!'

'Grammar school girl,' said Kilgrady. He leaned forward and whispered, 'What was all that crap she was readin'? For the love of Jaysus we could have been in the pub a quarter of an hour ago.'

'Christ, I know,' hissed Jamie. 'It wa' terrible, wa'n't it!'

'What's wrong wi' it? It's a beautiful story,' Dolly defended her friend. 'I liked it. She must be good because she's gettin' a story published.'

'Twice I nearly turned that telly up so loud that they'd be complainin' to her landlord from Risley Hill,' said Kilgrady.

'Shush, before she comes in an' bleddy 'ears yer,' Dolly told him.

About ten minutes later Julie came back. Her hair was tied in a pony tail with a red ribbon. She was now dressed in a frilly pink blouse and a bright red pleated skirt. They got their coats and came out of the flat after Julie had turned off the fire, telly and lamp. Outside the flat she closed the door and turned to lock it. Jamie looked at her slim neck and back; he'd been handed her for the night and if he played his cards right, he might have her for longer.

They went down the stairs and out to the van. Kilgrady unlocked the doors and they all got in. Until closing time they did the rounds of as many city pubs as there was time for.

The crowds were coming out of the pubs as they got into the van at the end of a gay evening. Julie and Jamie went in the back and Dolly sat next to Kilgrady. Dolly put the wireless on as they came slowly out of the car park into the road. Jamie hadn't drunk as much as Kilgrady and he hadn't drunk as much as Dolly but he had drunk much more than Julie and was now lying on his back with his head on Julie's lap, half alive.

Kilgrady pulled up outside 14 Lincoln Hill, the flats where Julie lived. They all went up to the second floor noisily. Julie unlocked her door and they went in. She closed the door, switched on the lamp, dropped her coat on the settee and wandered into the kitchenette to make some coffee—black coffee.

Jamie fell heavily on to the settee, behind the coffee table and took the lid off of the typewriter.

'Never had a goo on one o' these before,' he told them, his words slurred.

He banged out every letter, number and punctuation mark on the keyboard and then he realized that he had ruined a page of Julie's story.

'Heyup.' He pulled it out and looked at it, holding it up near his nose. 'Ah, not to worry. She's got some of 'ers left. It's better'n nowt.'

'You've ruined her lovely story,' Dolly said, like a child threatening to tell teacher.

'Don't tell 'er,' Jamie whispered. 'She'll not notice owt.'

'She will, 'cos you can't read it,' said Dolly.

'Yer can,' said Jamie, looking at the top of the page which hadn't been messed up. He began to read—too drunk to be able to see any letter less than twice. He couldn't pronounce words properly or understand them. Kilgrady and Dolly listened to Jamie as he entertained them until they looked up and saw Julie standing in the doorway with the tray of coffee and saucers in her hand.

'What muck,' Jamie was howling. 'The silly little girl wants to go to a writin' school. She wants to learn to write proper stories like that bloke Hemming, eh Dion? No real writer would write crap like that, would thee?'

Julie carried the tray across the room and put it on the open flap of the writing bureau. She sugared her own coffee and then sat in silence in the armchair with the cup in her hands. Jamie dropped the typed page and got up. He lurched towards the bureau and demanded loudly:

42

'Which is mine?' Nobody said anything. He bent down to Julie. 'Did y'ear me, love? Which is mine? I take it there *is* some for me, ent there? I mean, there's three cups there on the tray.'

Julie looked away and pulled the ribbon out of her hair, making her hair fall down on her shoulders. Jamie began to feel sick. He lurched towards the bureau, clutching the air, then sent the tray and everything on it crashing to the floor. Jamie retained his balance and stood, stunned, watching the widening pools of coffee and milk as they seeped into the carpet.

Dolly gave a shriek, Kilgrady let out a stream of abuse. Jamie just stood there, swaying.

'Ah'm sorry,' he choked. 'Honest I am. I didn't mean to do that.' He looked at Julie. 'Dirt like me should never o' come near you. I'm nowt—an' I wanted yer to think I was summat. But I'm not owt. I'm just a son of a bitch and a maniac who are only fit for each other. Fit for bringin' up a yob like me. Really you're a good little writer. Honest to Jesus you are.'

She said nothing. Jamie fell forward on to the carpet and lay still among the wreckage of the tray.

When Jamie opened his eyes again he found he had his arm around Kilgrady and was leaning all his weight on him. Facing him was Wilf Howe, in the doorway of a house with a yellow door and a door-knocker with a lion's face on it.

'Jamie!' cried Wilf.

'He went thatta way,' Jamie slurred. He looked down Kilgrady's earhole. 'Unsaddle me, sir.'

'Bring him through 'ere, mate,' Wilf roared. Kilgrady, supporting Jamie's full weight, followed Wilf through the house and out into the back garden. Wilf relieved Kilgrady of Jamie's weight and carried him to the bottom of the garden where he dropped him, unconscious, into the grass. 'Tharr'll teach the bogger not to come 'ome drunk.'

Halfway through the next morning Jamie became aware that he was being pushed and prodded. He opened his eyes, found the strain too much for him and closed them again. Rain was pouring down and he'd been sleeping among the fairies all through the cold night. The prodding and jabbing was persistent and after a time he opened his eyes again—not very wide—but wide enough to recognize the face of Kilgrady, with the world whizzing round and his head aching as if a house brick had just fallen on it. He had the most horrible, nasty, sickly taste in his mouth. He felt as if death were the thing he wanted most.

'Speak to me when you've rediscovered the English language,' said Kilgrady. He pulled Jamie up so that he was sitting with his back against the wall.

Jamie's mind wandered through fog and found the words, sorted out which order they should come in and spoke in a small gruff voice:

'Where am Ah?'

'In your back garden sleepin' off sumpin' like five or six pints,' grinned Kilgrady. 'I felt rough meself, this mornin'. Ah, sure, you'll get used to it.' The grin faded. 'You did more than your share of damage last night. You upset Julie Dean badly. Not only were you being rude to her, but you smashed to pieces her coffee set and made a mess of her carpet. I brought you home and your father said you were to lie out here. An' here you've lain all night.'

'I ought ter ge. . . .' Jamie's head couldn't take it. Every word he tried to say in a loud voice hurt him. Even if he nodded his head, something inside went *zing*! So he started

44

again, in a quiet voice: 'I ought to gerrin' that 'ouse an' tear the arse off that old man o' mine. Ooh!'

'Sure, it looks like you've been sick during the night,' Kilgrady said. 'It's a hell of a mess here.'

'Jesus Christ,' moaned Jamie, rubbing his heavy, aching head. 'An' it's rainin' too. I bet it's been slashin' down for hours.'

'It hasn't,' Kilgrady told him. 'Come on, now. Let's get out of it.'

'I could 'ave died here last night,' Jamie realized, shocked. 'Catch bloody pneumonia—or bronchitis—and I could kick the bucket. Bleedin' 'ell fire! That old man of mine'll get knifed in the brain one day, with luck.'

Kilgrady helped him up and slowly and unsteadily they made their way to the shed. Kilgrady gave him an outline of what he'd done at Julie's home the night before.

'So you'll have to go an' apologize to Julie and take her somethin' to show you're sorry.'

He went into the shed and came out again with a bunch of flowers and a box of chocolates.

'Lucky they sell flowers outside the cemetery on a Sunday,' he said.

'What's the flowers for?' Jamie inquired. 'We ain't gerrin' married, are we?'

'Give them to her!' Kilgrady said, firmly. 'You behaved like a pig. You showed your Kellowyn manners beautifully. Now look. So far she knows nottin' about you bein' in Kellowyn. There's five pounds in the chocolate box to cover the damage you did. You can give it me back at the end of the week when you come to meet Charlie. Here's her address,' and he handed Jamie a slip of paper.

Kilgrady went on to say, 'Julie's a nice girl and you were pure nasty.'

45

'You didn't stop me, did you!' moaned Jamie.

'Sure, was I sober meself?' argued Kilgrady. 'This is the least you can do. For the love of Jaysus, you can't begrudge her this!'

'I don't, Dion,' whimpered Jamie, shivering. 'I don't begrudge it 'er. Honest I don't. I think she's a nice girl too . . . I'd better get meself cleaned up.'

Jamie went to the back door and tried to open it but it hadn't been unlocked yet. So he pulled open the scullery window and climbed through. His head was throbbing.

He found himself the only person in the scullery. The cooker made the room hot, and in the comfort of the warmth he sat on the edge of the bath for a few minutes wondering what to do. Then he got up, unlocked the door, and went out to the shed. He came back with the flowers and chocolates, closed the door behind him and placed them on the table.

Jamie dug his hand in his pocket and pulled out a shilling for the bath geyser. He rammed the coin in the slot and turned everything on. As the water began pouring into the bath he searched through the cupboard to try to find something that would wash away the nasty taste in his mouth. Nothing would. So he stood at the sink rubbing his face with a cold flannel.

Wilf came in and looked him up and down.

'Heyup, this is a fine start, i'n't it?'

'Gerrout,' grunted Jamie. 'I'm gonner ey a bath. That's if I need one after lyin' out there in the rain catchin' me death o' cold. Thanks ter yo'.'

'I'm not 'avin' you roll in 'ere drunk at any time,' bellowed Wilf.

'Well you never gave me that complete list of rules, Dad, did yer?' said Jamie. 'You told me there was to be rules but

I never 'eard what any on 'em wa'. Yer went straight off out an' I ain't seen yer since. Do you realize I might be dead by the end o' this week?' He carried on rubbing the wet flannel around his heavy eyelids.

'You ain't eyin' a bath now,' Wilf told him. 'Your Mam's got ter get the dinner ready.'

Jamie threw the flannel in the sink and sat on the edge of the bath. 'I think the night I spent in the garden earned me this bath.'

'It earned you nowt,' snapped Wilf. 'But if you come back home drunk again it'll earn you nowhere to live. Now turn it off.'

Jamie turned the bath tap off. 'Well. We aren't going to get on very well with each other, are we? Da'!'

Wilf turned to go but his eyes caught the flowers and chocolates on the table. 'Wha's them for? Yer Mam don't like chocolates.'

'She don't like chocolates because God Almighty you don't like her to like chocolates,' snapped Jamie. 'I could tell you not ter be so nosey and to mind your own bleddy business but I ain't goin' to. They ain't for Mam.'

'Who are they for then?' Wilf asked.

'Get stuffed.'

'That Naemis hussey?'

'Lynn Naemis is Bob Denham's girl-friend, not mine. If you want to know, they're for another girl. A girl who you'd never meet in your flamin' life unless I brought her 'ome, which I wouldn't insult her by doin'.'

'The trouble wi' yo' is that you mix wi' the wrong kind o' people,' Wilf told him. 'It was a Mick what brought you 'ome last night.'

'Huh, and you mix wi' enough o' them yourself,' said Jamie.

'But I can tek me ale and keep me wits about me,' laughed Wilf. 'You should know that tripe like 'im'll get you sloshed to the eyebrows. I bet you only had three pints though. I could drink five times as much as you when I was younger than you.'

'So I can see by the size of that gut,' snapped Jamie. 'I cain't remember a time when you never had a pot belly. You've allus looked like a pregnant yak.'

Wilf moved as if to hit Jamie, but Dot came in and intervened.

'Oh, stop this arguin' and let me get on with the dinner.' Wilf went out and Jamie offered two fingers to his back.

That afternoon Jamie stood outside Julie's door, staring at the white letter J, straightening his tie. He could hear the noise of the typewriter and knew she must be writing. Two minutes later he plucked up courage and rang the doorbell. Julie opened the door, dressed as she had been the first time she had opened it the evening before. This time she wasn't smiling. She looked annoyed.

'Heyup,' he said, a little nervously. 'I've come to apologize. I woke up this mornin'—yer know—feelin' generally hung up—yer know—feelin' like I'd been hanged, taken down, hanged, taken down and hanged again. I'd—I'd really like to apologize. Wi' these.'

She didn't even look at the flowers or the box of chocolates. She stood aside so he could go in. The sun was shining into the bright room. The television was off and the record player was playing softly. Jamie looked at the patch in the carpet where Julie had obviously been trying to clean up the stain.

'The music's to try and calm me down,' she said with a note of bitterness in her voice. 'All I've been able to do with

48

my characters is to have the hero knock the heroine around with his fists in a room as small as this.'

Jamie felt uncomfortable. 'It ain't small. All the rooms at 'ome are smaller and scruffy. It's in a bad part of Nottingham and . . . I didn't mean whatever I said, Julie. You've got to believe that because it's gospel truth. An' I'd 'ad too much to drink.' He held out the flowers and chocolates. 'There's money in the chocolate box to pay for the damage. I hope it will cover the damage and mend it up between us. We got on okay last night until I got myself into a disgusting state and spoiled it all.'

She took them from him. 'Thanks, Jamie. The flowers are lovely. But you can have the money back. The coffee set was a Christmas present from my mother. You can't buy sentimental value.'

Jamie looked out of the window into the garden of grass, shrubs and flowers which faced a clean, quiet, sunny street. Jamie had stepped out of Borstal. And he'd been hurt in those three free days as many times as he'd been hurt in the two years inside. And he'd hurt other people, too. His only friends were those who had been taken from the backstreets, been caught running through fields pursued by police for crimes they had committed. All little rebels who took chances to show their hatred of people, from their side of the institution gates. Everybody must have been a rebel in Kellowyn. Jamie thought there was at least an ounce of rebel in each one of them. Everybody hates, only I hate more than anybody else, he told himself. I hate most people because people are the only beings that steal, cheat, blackmail and murder. They do it to you so you must do it back to them— before somebody cheats you and steals from you, before you're blackmailed and murdered, yourself. Two long years I've been thinking about nothing but rebelling. Not that I'll ever be able to do anything flashy. But I'm a rebel, like most people of my caste in life, and they, like me, haven't the courage to rebel outwards. They keep it all inside. But I won't try telling Julie any of that. She mightn't understand.

What *would* Julie understand? He didn't know a thing about her—and he wanted to know everything there was to know. He wanted to become so close to her that she would wind up needing him. Yet what could he offer a girl like Julie?

'Perhaps we could find out where yer mother bought the coffee set an' goo an' get another one?' he suggested falteringly as Julie put on another record.

'No,' said Julie. 'I think she got it in London . . . it doesn't matter.'

'Anyway, keep the fiver—it'll help pay off the rent for this place.'

She sat back in the armchair, leaving Jamie the settee. 'My father pays most of the rent. He owns three television shops outside Nottingham.'

'Don't you go to work then?'

'Yes, I work in a wool shop four mornings a week, but I don't earn much there. Fortunately my parents understand me and they help.'

'Get on wi' yer Mam an' Dad then, do yer?' he asked.

'Yes,' said Julie. 'Why shouldn't I?'

He shrugged his shoulders. 'No reason.'

'Don't you mek out with yours?'

He didn't answer that for a few seconds. Then,

'No. It's me old man. You see, I wish he was dead. It's as simple as that. I 'ate 'is guts.'

'Why?'

'I 'ate his guts for bringin' me Mam to a bad area in Nottingham from a good area in Derby,' said Jamie. 'I 'ate 'is guts mainly for bringin' her to Deighton Street. You see Deighton Street is a turning off of Tennon Street. I 'ate Tennon Street almost as much as I 'ate the old feller. I never got on with him. It wouldn't be so bad if we didn't live where we do. "The hidden streets", I call 'em. Nobody'll ever tell you where they are and how to get to them because they're dirty and they've produced a good part of the county's crooks. The whole place smells of rotten eggs. Tennon Street is where they want to get the bulldozers. They should knock that down and build a new beautiful street with beautiful houses with beautiful gardens and trees and flowers with two big bright signs—one at each end of Tennon Street—reading:

> At last—PARADISE WAY, Nottingham's Pride.
> Let the past be buried.

'The men on Tennon Street have a motto. So they can take life easy and have an excuse they say, "You dream about careers, but out of your imagination and dreams' reach, you end up slogging your guts out in a factory". And that's their excuse for not getting on in life.'

'Why do you stay if you dislike it so much?' she asked.

Cornered, Jamie snapped at himself. Like to tell her about those two years stuck in Kellowyn? And why you were put there in the first place? What about saying: Julie, I haven't been about Tennon Street much lately because I got purraway for doin' summat little boys shouldn't do. I raped a sixteen-year-old girl, I stole forty-eight nicker and I fiddled the fruit machines. Anyroad, after I got me guts kicked in by the blokes in charge, the Guv said to 'issen, 'You can stop kickin' Howe's guts in now, Bernie, 'e's out next wik. You better find him a job in that slum Nottingham, nice an' near 'is 'ome.' So it's like that. I'm stuck with Curris's job and I'll 'ate it, by Christ I will.

Jamie laughed bitterly to himself. No, he couldn't tell Julie that. Then he said aloud:

'I s'pose I cain't leave me old lady alone wi' 'im. Not yet I'll 'ave ter stay around for a bit.'

'Have you any brothers or sisters?'

'You're kiddin',' laughed Jamie. 'As it was *I* was a mistake. Have you?'

'No, I haven't.'

'So you live alone here, do you?'

'Yes.'

'Don't yer get lonely—sometimes?'

'No. I like being alone,' Julie replied and got up quickly, as if to end the subject. 'Would you like some tea?' she said.

'Isn't that askin' too much—after last night?'

She smiled and went into the kitchenette.

Julie had deliberately cut short her answer to Jamie's question because she could never bring herself to tell him the truth. He wouldn't understand it, no one did; even her parents, though sympathetic, were puzzled by it. Dolly was a loyal friend, but had no depth of understanding.

The most important thing in Julie's life was her writing. It may be bad and worthless but she *had* to do it. It was the only *real* thing. She lived alone with the characters of her stories. They were real to her. The rest of the world outside her flat was plastic.

Julie had never made friends easily. She didn't like parties because she was always nervous about meeting groups of people. Once she knew the people and had settled in the crowd she usually felt better and then didn't have to search desperately for words.

It was at a party that she had first met Dion Kilgrady.

Another boy who had taken her had left her on her own. He hadn't come back. Kilgrady had strolled across the room, with his usual confident grin, to chat up the new shy girl. He had introduced her to his friends there, including Dolly whom she knew slightly because Dolly worked in one of her father's shops. Since then she'd often gone out with them, but on the whole her life was solitary.

Julie would have liked a *real* friend. Someone to communicate with. Someone she could talk to who would listen without laughing and would understand when she had finished. Boy or girl, it didn't matter. She wasn't interested in a sex relationship—just a friend whom she could value high above the characters she created. But until she met such a person, she'd be content to go on as she was.

While Julie was in the kitchenette, Jamie leaned forward to read what she had just been writing. By the coffee table was a plastic waste-paper basket. It was filled with typed paper that had been screwed up and torn.

The record faded. The room was silent, except for a humming noise coming from the idle record player.

If only he could try and look at Julie and her writing the way she did. And he knew he had to, although he wasn't sure why so early in their relationship. He knew that she might be pleased with him if he took an interest in every part of her; her way of life, her home, her background, her family and, most of all, her writing.

The page in her typewriter was headed:

LEAD ME ON THEN LET ME DIE
by Julie Dean

He read what followed and made himself like what he read. There were only three paragraphs but the next he knew was a hand pulling it out of the machine, screwing it up and dropping it into the wastepaper basket.

Jamie looked up. 'Why d'yer do that? It was the makings of a good story.'

'Please,' said Julie, putting a cup of tea on the table before him. 'Don't talk about my writing. You don't like it, and you don't have to pretend to.'

'But I do,' shouted Jamie. 'I want to read some more . . . Can I borrow some of it?' Then he added nervously, 'Will you let me? P'raps that novel Dolly was tellin' me about. I'm sure it ud be interestin'.'

Julie sat down next to him on the settee. Suddenly he felt embarrassed and even less confident than when he had first met her. Should he make love to her? He didn't particularly want to. He didn't think he could anyway.

'I know I've got a cheek comin' around here and showin' me ugly puss,' he said. 'But I can't be sorrier. Honest.'

'Put another record on,' she said.

FOUR

The juke box played on in the café on Tennon Street as Don Gordon and Tommy Bryan ate their tea. No one tried to talk above the noise and Tommy buried himself in his paper from time to time.

Don thought, 'No I don't like music when I'm tryin' ter think. An' now I've got somethin' to think about.' He'd hoped he would never see Jamie Howe again, to be able to forget Val Harpe, the stolen money, the police, the whole bloody business. But now it would all be dragged up. Now he could never feel safe with Jamie Howe a few doors away.

He'd have to move out and live somewhere else. Back to London perhaps, where he'd spent part of his childhood. He could still hear Jamie's cutting, 'Do yer still cry in public places?' No, he didn't, not now. He'd got used to not having friends—he didn't care any more. And it was when he'd got around to not caring that he'd met Tommy, and they'd been together for about six weeks now. He didn't want to bust things up with Tommy—though Jamie Howe would probably do that for him.

The only good that had come out of the Val Harpe mess-up was that it had given him one friend. Funny sort of friend, too—the Probation Officer. For a year he'd had to go and see Mr. Ronald Harrison every Thursday night. Harrison hadn't treated him like dirt; he'd talked to him, and asked him about himself. Somehow it was easy talking to Mr.

Harrison. He was never in a hurry to get rid of him and Don had, over the months, told him everything that had been boiling up inside for years.

In Ronald Harrison's office over endless cups of tea, Don had told him a story which, when put together, went something like this:

Like you know, I was born here in the Robin Hood county of Nottinghamshire. Robin Hood! Now there was a nutcase. I doubt very much that there was any such bloke in Lincoln green with a bow and arrow who led a gang of merrie men about. For a start I don't see what they had to be so bloody merry about. Sherwood Forest couldn't have been no paradise, especially in winter. All that, just to feed the poor.

Nobody is that charitable these days and I bet you a quid they weren't in them days, either. Even if Robin Hood existed I bet he was a right drunken sod and his men were about as merrie as the Mafia. Grizzly-looking killers, drunk all the time.

Do you know how Nottingham got its name? You'll laugh when I tell you. Thousands of years ago this tribe-leader had his tribe on the bank of the Trent and his name was Snot—all right, don't believe me then—and so they called the town Snottingaham. I don't know why they changed it but I've got a pretty good idea.

I reckon I've been crossing the gods all my life as did my old man before me but then there was nobody on Tennon Street who had much luck. I left school last year hating people because all the while I'd been in school—in London and Nottingham—people had kept on telling us we'd find the world was cruel and harsh. Over and over they'd tell us and I'd get all worked up behind my desk and I was sure that one day I'd stand up and knock books and ink pots, pens and papers flying all over the room and yell back, 'We know, we know, we bloody well know because you keep bleedin' tellin' us every five minutes.' I reckon they should all have shut up because I knew how cruel the world was as much as them teachers—if not better. I also knew *why* it was cruel. It's only *people* that make it cruel. Plain, simple-minded bloody people. And I wasn't having any Youth Employment Officer nudging me about for the simple reason that I didn't have the foggiest idea what I was going to do when I left school, and I told them I didn't much care either.

I followed my late father's clod-hopping footsteps because there wasn't a trade within reach that I fancied, so now I'm a bleedin' labourer. And it wouldn't be so bad if I was old enough to booze in the pub but I ain't and I'll be here in this factory, clocking in every day, for the next fifty years. There was a time when I had hopes, dreams, ambitions. I was good at drawin' and paintin'. Maybe I could have been an artist—but confidence and happiness are easily washed down the drain. Mine were the day my old man got killed.

I can still see my dad's guts wrapped round the steering wheel of a wrecked car near Epping Forest. I can see me trotting home, going upstairs, sitting on the bed and looking out of the window trying to cry for him. But I couldn't. Because I hated my father and so did my mother. Some superstitious nutcase once told me that kids pick their parents before they're born. Work that one out! Well if that's true I must be more bloody stupid than I thought I was. It can't be true, anyroad, because if that was how things happened the old man would have had to go up into the mountains, a hermit, because nobody would have asked to be a child of his, and I don't remember many people who went much on him when he was here. It hadn't taken my old lady many years to go off him, but she'd kept with him for my sake, she said.

After four years in Walthamstow, mam and me came back to Tennon Street and I had to go into the James Ruffnall School to serve my last year. What we came back to Nottingham for I don't know.

I didn't want to know the kids at Ruffnall much. I don't get on with people. I'm a big social problem. I never went to bed before half past eleven at night and always set the alarm for six. Tennon Street is cold, wet, deserted and dark as I look down from the upstairs rooms we live in. Rain has fallen during the night but now it has stopped. Just across the road is a street light—but in Nottingham the street lights go off at midnight. Not like London where the lights are on until the sun gets up.

I rise out of the mattress like a zombie, my hair all tangled and looking like a haystack. I'm the only one awake in the house. Mam's asleep and the Beharns, downstairs, are also asleep. They don't exist at that time of the morning. Nothing is alive but me. I'm the only thing that exists. And a few hours later I'm behind my desk in a classroom finding out that too many people do exist. No matter what time I get up I feel like there's two sacks of soil weighing my eyelids down.

At school I was happy about sweet nothing and I knew I hadn't any ideas for a job when summer popped around. I was miserable all the time and the more miserable you feel the more miserable you make yoursen. Loneliness helps this too. Yet being as I'm self-centred—as a teacher said—I didn't particularly want mates.

The only person I wanted to know was a girl in the class who I'd fallen for. She was about the only person who said 'hello' to me. And she always smiled when she said it. I sort of wished that this was because she fancied me, but inside I knew that she was just intrigued by my character as a lonely, lost boy who sits behind his desk reading, drawing with a pencil, sleeping or just sitting thinking. I knew how different I was from the others—never mixed with gangs, never talked to anyone—and I hated myself for it. But I couldn't do a thing about it. I only ever spoke or smiled at this girl. Her name was Linda and I was miserable inside knowing I'd never get as far as taking her out. And since I met her, I listened to the words of every sad song I heard.

> *Do you wonder about me*
> *Like I'm hoping you do?*
> *Are you lonesome without me?*
> *Have you found someone new?*

Sometimes I listened to that song for a whole evening. Just playing it and replaying it until I could only hear it in the background and I had my whole mind concentrating on Linda. I told myself: she leaves at Easter and you leave at summer so be bloody quick if you want a date with her. You'll never have her though because life doesn't work that way. You'd have anything and everything to live for if you had her but you ain't and you never will have, so help me God all-bleedin'-mighty! You think she's good-looking, pleasant, polite and all the rest of it. But if she knew what was riding through your mind she'd sit down with the rest of Ruffnall and laugh like nobody laughed before.

> *All my dreams of Linda*
> *Have been burnt to a cinder.*
> *I'm dead in her mind*
> *Yet she's lovely and kind.*

I started going through days of depression and then weeks, and even Mam started getting worried about me. She never particularly bothered much before and she hardly meant any more to me than the old feller did. But I'll give her her due: she'd step in whenever dad got mad and went for me, and she'd taken some lashings over it in her time. But she never encouraged me once in my life. One teacher wrote in a report that I was withdrawn and introverted and that I needed encouragement from home—particularly where art was concerned. Well, me mam didn't know what they was talkin' about—she didn't know *what* I could do. Mind you, I bet I would have left home if she'd started encouraging me all of a sudden. I wouldn't have been able to get used to it.

The thought of rambling about appealed to me. I fancied the colourful life of hitch-hiking about the countryside. I could see myself going from place to place looking for something I could never find—something that always looked like Linda. I'd clear out next week if I had the money and if I wasn't on probation and booked to come and see you, Mr. Harrison, once every week for the next year.

Friday evening and the cold bitter wind would blow through me as I'd stand on Stony Clouds, five miles out of the city, on the edge of Nottinghamshire and Derbyshire, thinking how beautiful it would be if I could bring Linda up these grassy hills. I'd stand her on the rocks for all the M.1 motorists to see as they drove past. The motorway didn't make any difference to the peacefulness of Stony Clouds.

I never really knew what love was because I'd never been in love. I'd never loved family or relations. But this must have been the right feeling with Linda. What everybody in books, films and on telly talks about. Them lot make me laugh, though. Not talking normal. Putting on false voices what they think sounds sexy, but just don't seem lifelike to me. Not that I can sit in a room for long with a telly that's flashin' love and kisses because all that love-tripe they bung on the box just ain't real. The blokes who write these plays don't even begin to understand love. Their only aim is to make money, but they shouldn't write about what they don't understand. Love is something to understand—not that I understand it—but at least I try to. There must be something more to it than they make out on the box with a bloke and a tart rolling about in bed with just their bare shoulders showing and their lips going all over their ugly chops.

But what would I know about it all? How can I talk when I've only been in love and was never loved in return?

Don't think I sat around and looked miserable *all* the time because the more I realized that soon Linda would be getting up and going, never to return to that desk in the formroom again, the more I made up my mind to try *something* before it was too late. But she was never alone. She knocked about with a girl called Marie Maitland, who was also in our class. At dinner times they usually went shopping for their mothers up New Tennon Street. Straight out of school I would race up to New Tennon Street and then on to Housenal Street, then turn and take a slow walk back towards Tennon Street. This was so I'd walk into the girls who would probably be looking at fruit and veg. outside a greengrocer's shop or at L.P.s on a rack outside the record shop. I'd say 'hello' to them. Linda would look up and smile, 'Oh, hello, Don,' but Marie wouldn't speak. Then they'd walk on by, and I'd go in the café.

One Friday Marie was away. It was near the end of term and at dinner time I rushed up to Housenal, then slowly back the way I came. My heart split in two when I saw Linda carrying a shopping bag and looking in shop windows

61

as she walked towards me. I was standing near the café door when she brushed my shoulder—apparently not noticing me—and I turned and called, 'Hello, Linda!' Christ, it was the first time I'd found courage to call her by her name. Then I said, 'Not talkin' terday, aren't yer?'

She looked over her shoulder. 'Oh, 'eyup!' And she hurried on up New Tennon Street, not even stopping to go into the co-op. I felt awful as I sat in the café at the table in the corner, I'm that unnoticeable, eh? 'Oh, 'eyup!' Not, 'Oh, 'eyup, Don.' Still, she looked like she was in a hurry and—I lied to myself—if I'd been in a hurry I wouldn't have noticed her either.

The juke box was playing, but I hardly heard it. I sat there thinking it had all been a mistake. Linda's 'hello' in school had meant nothing. She didn't even know I existed. I must have been a bit on the mental side to wonder if I could ever get her to go out wi' me. Too many people laugh at me, I was thinking. And don't kid yersen. Donovan boy, I bet she does too.

The few times any of the girls had made a date with me, I'd been led right up the garden path. They'd ask you for a date. You don't really want to go out wi' 'em but you turn up to the place arranged just to see if they will and they're never there. They're behind some brick wall having a bloody good laugh with their real boy friend. Or else you get, ''Ey Don, Maggie wants a date wi' yer.' And when you turn round to see what Maggie looks like Maggie cries, 'Oo no, it i'n't me as wants a date wi' yer, it's 'er.' But, I told myself, Linda's not like that. She'd not pull any rotten stunts.

I sat in that café letting me tea get cold. I couldn't touch it—it'd choke me. Then I looked up at the clock and saw, coming in the doorway, a girl in a dark green school blazer. It was Linda—walking straight towards me. The people

62

never moved, the clock hand never moved, the record on the turntable never moved, the needle never moved—the juke was still. Linda smiled, put her bag on the floor, unbuttoned her blazer and caught her breath. 'Phew! Heyup Don.' Then the people were alive again, the hands on the clock moved and the record played.

I didn't know what to say. I opened my mouth an' all that would come out was a silly American, 'Hiya.' Then I managed to say, 'Si' down, love.'

'Hold on,' she said. 'I'm just goin' ter gerracup o' tea.'

'No—sit down and I'll get it for you,' I volunteered.

'It's all right, I'll get it.'

'Don't be silly,' I said, now on my feet. 'Sit down.'

'Thanks,' she said, offering a sixpence and a threepenny bit.

'Hang on to it,' I told her. 'I've got a bit of spare cash.'

'No, Don,' she insisted. 'Tek it.'

'I said it's all right, didn't I?' I cried.

'Tek the bleddy money,' she said, sticking it in my blazer pocket. Well, I couldn't have imagined her mate Marie, or anybody else, forcing money on me. Marie would have said something like, 'Oh, sod yer then. Nobody can say I didn't offer.' Anyroad, I got Linda her tea out of her own money.

'On your own, then, today?' I said, watching her sugar the tea.

'Ah. Marie's down wi' flu,' she told me. 'Christ, Don, to-day you've said the most I've ever heard you say. You're always quiet and on yer own, aren't you?' I shrugged my shoulders. 'Are you ill or summat?'

'You don't 'ave to worry about me, Linda. Nobody else does,' I said, and in case she thought I was trying to get sympathy I added, 'and that suits me fine.'

'Don't you go out with any of your mates at night?' she asked.

'I a'n't gorrany mates,' I told her. 'At night I walk the streets by mesen if they're dark enough. And around 'ere they usually are.'

'Why are you so lonely then?' Linda questioned. 'What's up?'

'Nowt.'

'Come off it, there must be summat wrong,' Linda insisted, sipping her tea. 'People are mekin' some nasty jokes up about you at school. Even the teachers. You oughto smile once in a while.' What she'd said didn't make me feel like smiling, and when she saw I still looked miserable a big smile came across her face—she looked lovely when she smiled, too. When I smile I look worse than when I don't.

'What you need is a night out somewhere gay,' Linda went on. 'Somewhere not around here. I know what helps you look sad. Tennon Street and all round here—it's enough to sadden anybody. But what can you do but get used to it?'

'You'll be left school soon, won't you?' I said. 'Next week.'

'Hm,' said Linda. 'I'm gettin' a job downtown, I not be workin' around here. Thank God. What are yo' gonner do when you leave? Leave at summer or Easter?'

'Easter?' I cried. 'I should be so lucky.'

'Never mind,' she smiled. 'Eager to gerrout are you?'

'Aye, an' I only miss it by four days.'

'I only just get in,' she said. 'What do you intend to do when your turn pops round?'

'Ah, just kick about the place,' I shrugged my shoulders. 'I wanted to be an artist before—when I was younger . . .'

'Oh, I've seen some of your pictures in the art room,' she told me. 'I think they're good. They look like a lot of work's gone into 'em. You must be gifted, they're so real. Especially that one of the girl standing against the horizon with

64

the sun settin' in an orange and purple sky—and you got that sky so real it's unbelievable. You can tell there's a breeze blowing through the girl's long hair. It's lovely.'

Well, honest, I'd never been flattered so much in all my life! Never! And she was the only person I wanted words like that from. Not from the art teachers, not from the form master and not from me mam. Just from Linda.

'Thank you very much,' I said. 'That's very nice of you. But all ambitions and hopes got washed down the plughole years ago when I saw me Dad smash himself up in a car accident. Seen him drive off in his nice shiny car, going out to have a drink. I wen' out and saw 'im dead.'

She wasn't smiling now. 'I'm sorry.'

'Don't be, 'cos I bleddy well wasn't and neither was my mam,' I told her. 'In fact, whenever I saw him drive off I always felt like yelling, "I hope you crash it and get killed." Three hours later me an' my cousin were walkin' along a road near Epping Forest and we saw this car smashed up round a lamp-post with coppers standin' around, ambulance —the lot. It was his car and his remains were glued to the steering wheel, pinned there by the wreckage and seat. The coppers tried to keep me away, but I dodged round them— I wanted to see 'im. I was as sick as a dog. I went home and I tried to cry, as I sat on my bed, but I couldn't wet a tear for him. Only for the terrible sight of seeing a person in that state. It gives you a shock and no matter who you see like it you wished to hell you hadn't. If I'd only heard about his death and not seen it, it wouldn't have been the same. But seein' a person end this way—yer can't forget it.'

I realized I must have made Linda feel uncomfortable be-cause how could she say she was sorry when I'd told her this? She couldn't say, 'Oh, that's good,' either, so I went on:

'You're the only real friend I've got in this school or out.'

I wanted to say: when you leave school I'll feel all the loneliness I should have felt when Dad died. But I couldn't bring myself to say it. I thought that no matter how true it was, it was going a bit too far.

She sighed and looked sorry for me. Then she looked irritated. 'Why do they play such rotten loud music?' She meant the juke box, what else?

When the last disc faded I was up to the slot 'n' buttons before any other teenager or lorry driver could get there with 'is tanners and I popped two bobs' worth of tanners in the juke and pressed four buttons, turning on the quieter music. I sat back beside her and she grinned as the first record dropped and began to play. 'That's better. The other stuff was beginning to play a headache into my brain.'

I tried not to think she had shaken me off the subject. So like a nut I spat out, 'Before you leave can I tek you out? Once! Please. I'll not tek you out around here. Downtown where all the good places are. I'll take you to the Odeon or the A.B.C. and a posh restaurant after. I'll pay for it all. Them restaurants are nice. Open late to cater for the crowds comin' out of pictures, pubs and theatres. Just one date!'

'I dunno,' she said, looking uncertain, and finished her tea.

The sound of Linda's cup being replaced on its saucer sounded fifty times louder than it really was. Again, the people never moved, the clock hands never moved, the record on the turntable never moved; everything was still, everything was silent. Then, after a hundred years of sleep, the world woke up. Linda smiled faintly and said,

'Yeh. But you don't have to go mad. I don't mind just poppin' over the road to the Classic or the Envoy.'

I nearly fell off of the stool backwards. Honest to sweet lovable Jesus Christ I did. A hot fountain inside me shot

66

upwards and I didn't care two fingers for what was going on in the little world around me. All I cared about was Linda. I promised her a wonderful night out downtown and never even thought that I didn't have the money—nor did my mam—to pay for even one of us doing the things I promised. We arranged to meet on the following Friday at the point where New Tennon Street runs into Tennon Street. This would be her last day at school and I felt honoured that she should hand me this important night of hers. It was now my important night too.

That afternoon I surprised the form master and the kids in class by bouncing into the classroom as merry as a clown. Cracking jokes and grinning happily and making even them laugh friendly laughs. I got a punishment essay off one teacher because the silly whore got tired of my funny-funny comments, and even though I had to write two pages on 'Humour' I joked on and finally got sent out.

At quarter past six on the following Monday morning I was washing myself at the sink in the dark when it hit me like a bullet between the teeth that I didn't have the money to take Linda out with. Not to take her out the way I wanted and to create the right impression. I didn't have it, mam wouldn't have it, there was nobody I could borrow it off, and I had five days to get it.

I came into the classroom. Linda was at her desk next to Marie, again. I sat in my usual lonely spot behind two boys, one of whose name was Main. He turned to look at me. 'Heyup youth, you still bein' bitten by the funny bug or did you manage to kill it over the week-end?'

'Leave him, Mainiac,' the boy next to him said. 'You know he don't like anybody talkin' to him.'

'I'm okay,' I told him. 'Everything's all right now.'

I went through the day, the day after, the day after that, and the day after that with laughing, joking and getting quite friendly with Main and the rest of the lads who I'd thought I hated. But things were different now. Everything was all right.

Friday dinner time came around and I sat on the edge of the bed counting the seven and sixpence I had. This was all I had to take Linda out on. Seven and six would just about get us in a good seat at the pictures if we walked downtown and went without dudoos an' ices an' suckers and went without fish and chips and milk-shake or coke on our way home. And it would mean walking back in darkness to the Tennon Street area.

I live, as I said, in the upstairs rooms of a house on the lower part of Tennon Street where it looks all slummy. Mam and me live upstairs while the landlady, Mrs. Beharn, and her very old father live downstairs. There's a room with a bath and a sink in it, and the carsey is outside. So whenever me or the old girl gets the signal we have to go downstairs, through Ma Beharn's kitchen, out into the garden and into this white-walled toilet. If you want the bog to flush you have to yank the chain about seven times before you get a splutter out of it. They're all the same in this part of the street.

Well, after counting me seven and six I put it in me back pocket and went downstairs to go to the toilet and I came into Mrs. Beharn's kitchen. She wasn't about but I could see she'd just come in because her shopping bag was on the table packed with groceries. Sitting on the top of it all was a white shiny purse. Temptation clobbered me and as I faced the grim carsey wall I thought about the purse sitting on top of the world waiting for somebody to waltz in empty-handed and waltz out a few bob better off. Not that old Ma Beharn could have much dosh, I reckoned. I slammed the bog door behind me and stepped back into the kitchen. Well, it was still there. There was nobody about to see me if I pinched it. I stood wondering for a few minutes. I had promised Linda a good time and seven and six wouldn't provide that. Linda wouldn't want to know me if I took her downtown on seven and six. And I could slip Mrs. Beharn the money back during the month. That purse could help me to live for something. The next moment I could only believe the purse was mine and, before I realized I was thinking like a lunatic, I was lying back on my bed, breathing heavily and clutching the purse. I heard my mother coming along the landing so I stuffed it under the pillow.

On my way back to school I counted out three quid and zipped it up in me back pocket. Linda and I were going to have a fine night after all. And inside I felt a little hollow and wondered how I was gonner go about it. Would I get to hold her hand? Would I get to kiss her? And would I know how to kiss her properly? But I tried to dismiss these worries and sang songs to myself through the afternoon until three-thirty when the school was let out early and the leavers were wished good luck.

I looked into the cracked mirror after tea and thought to mesen, Flippin' 'ell! You must be jokin'. You mean to tell yourself that Linda wants to go out with *you*? Well I had to pluck up courage and rehearse lines that I might say to her. All through tea I tried it, speaking to myself in case mam heard. What I was saying sounded silly and if I'd ever said any of these things to Linda it would have been a crazy thing to do. An' all the while mam's goin' on about Mrs. Beharn losing her purse with all her money in while she was out shopping. But it was all right by me if the nutty cow thought she'd lost it out.

I stood in the bedroom, in front of the mirror, combing my hair and putting a dab of that Flame-thrower poncescent on to kill the smell of bad breath. I 'adn't got any really good clothes. Not many of the Ruffnall kids wore the school uniform. I was one of those who didn't. My school stuff was just jeans, white shirt and a pullover. And I didn't want to turn up in old school clothes that Linda had seen me in since September. I imagined mesen done up all good with a coloured silk shirt, cuff-links, black shoes and a well-cut suit. But the best I could do was a white shirt, desert boots and grey trousers. The trousers were a bit short and I must have looked a bit Yankified in them. I put my jacket on, stuffed the dosh in my pocket and walked up Tennon Street towards New Tennon Street. Suddenly I began to panic and hurried my steps, thinking she might not be there.

But she was. She was standing on the spot we had arranged, looking down Tennon Street for me. I gulped and tried not to feel too nervous as I approached her. She looked done up and was smiling.

'Hey—heyup,' I stammered, shrugging my shoulders.

'Hello Don,' she said. 'Where we off?'

'City centre,' I said. 'I've got a healthy bit of cash to-night.'

We walked up New Tennon Street and hopeless me was lost for words. I let her talk. We caught a bus from Housenal Street, and she told me how she was starting her new job next Wednesday. She pointed the place out as we went by it on the bus.

We got off at the city centre and walked to the nearest picture house. Linda took hold of my hand as we looked at the coloured stills in the glass cage and I cursed myself. Fancy me letting her do all the talking, and leaving her to grab hands.

'Do you fancy it then?' I asked her.

'It's up to you,' she told me.

'The 'ell it is,' I cried. 'It's your big day today.'

'All right, duck,' she grinned. 'Le's goo in an' see this.'

We joined the queue and I decided that we'd sit in the balcony. That set me back twelve bob for a starter. Then I bought her a six-bob box of chocolates which she never stopped thanking me for till half of the first film was over and then she kept offering them to me. My arm was beginning to get cramp with her leaning on it but I felt good to have her head on my shoulder and her hair against my neck and some of my cheek. I felt happy enough to squeeze her. Excitement thundered about inside me, bursting to jump out and kiss her, but I couldn't find courage enough to do that.

When the lights came on in the interval she told me that her father would be picking us up at ten o'clock with his car. He'd give me a lift home. I was sort of disappointed. I had wanted to take her to this Yankee-bar place on Upper Parliament Street for a milk-shake or a coke and a hot dog or hamburger after coming out of the pictures. I had wanted to walk her home from the bus stop on Housenal Street, through the dark streets so that she'd hold on to me tight for comfort in case any of the bully sods of Ruffnall, or the twisted-minded nutters, lurched out from behind a garden wall or dark entry. And besides, we might have been able to have a goodnight kiss, though I knew I'd boob that.

'No, Lin,' I told her. 'He needn't give me a lift 'ome. I'm fine walkin'.'

'Don't be daft, Don,' she cried. 'He'll not mind.'

'I want ter walk, anyroad,' I said. 'I'll bus it to Housenal and walk 'ome from there.'

'That's bleddy silly,' she told me. 'Me dad can drive you all the way home and it won't cost you owt.'

'It's only a tanner fare,' I said. I didn't want her or her old man to see the Stonehenge I live in.

'Well at least let him drop you off at the end of New Tennon Street,' she said.

'Here's the ice tart,' I told her. 'Want a sucker or a tub?'

'You've bought enough, Don,' she said firmly.

'I'll get a fruit tub then, will I?' I said, and with that I was up and out of my seat to the ice-cream woman.

We left half-way through the next film because I thought it was bloody awful and Linda had missed most of it because she'd gone to sleep using my shoulder as a pillow. We walked up the hill from Slab Square to Upper Parliament Street and found this bar. Both of us had a hamburger which was about one-and-nine each. That wasn't bad, being as you had to fork out half-a-crown for one at those hot dog and hamburger stalls in the West End of London. Linda had a strawberry milk-shake and I had a chocolate one. We sat at a clean table. There was only a few other couples in there and everything was quiet but for the sound of the traffic and the occasional pot-banging that went on behind the counter, coming from the kitchen. I thought the place looked right American. Modern-looking, but posh like some of the West End places. No yobs, no tramps. Just a few couples.

You could look out of the big window and watch the lights and traffic reflections of Upper Parliament Street. We looked up at the big white building that was the Theatre Royal and I said:

'They'll all be comin' in here out of there in a bit. It all reminds me of the West End in a small sort of way. I suppose it's this bar what makes me think about that. Right now I can see the neon lights of Piccadilly Circus. Whizzing around and changing pattern. The smell of hot dogs and hamburgers mingling with the night air. So many people dashing about. All of them so different and half of them American tourists going from one place to another and nobody but me noticing the electric lights. Haymarket is just off of Piccadilly Circus and I can remember standing there for about an hour, one Saturday night, watching them fantastic lights as I listened to a lot of nice records being played in a nearby record shop. It was last year. I'd been walking about that way in the sunshine since half past two in the afternoon. I lived in Walthamstow, in East London, and I got the train down to Liverpool Street, like every week-end. Then a tube train from Liverpool Street to Piccadilly and I walked around Piccadilly and Leicester Square and Soho, watching buskers, watching the crowds and it was a good day. I stayed until it was dark and then at ten o'clock I went home. It's marvellous, Lin. Maybe, one day, me and you can go down there. On a Saturday if you liked. We'd ey a great time, honest to God, we would.'

'I've had a great time tonight, Don,' she smiled, screwing her hamburger paper up. 'Thanks very much. You've spent a lot of money.'

'I a'n't spent owt yet,' I said modestly. 'Oops! Burnt me bleddy tongue on the 'ole 'amburger. Ent thee 'ot, eh?'

She laughed. 'You've changed a lot in this past week. Before last Fridee I wouldn't have imagined you as you are now. Talkin' away—happy and smiling. After all them months seeing a miserable lad behind his desk, all lonely.'

I grinned. 'All aloof like the gel in me horizon picture, eh? Ah, I think I'll call it that an' all, "Girl Aloof".'

'Oh, that's a beautiful picture,' she complimented me further. 'Call it summat romantic. Not "Girl Aloof" for Christ's sake! "Sunset Over the Horizon" or summat like that. You shouldn't o' gen up hope of bein' an artist like that, yer know.'

Sometimes I like talking about me being an artist as if the dream could ever have come true, but there was times when I thought it was pointless and didn't want to talk about it; this was one of them. I dropped it by saying, 'Glad you've left school, then?'

'I've left,' is what she said, and started sucking the pink, frothy strawberry milk up the straw.

'Aren't you happy?' I asked, seriously.

'It meks no difference,' she said. 'I'd like to stay on just to have a bash at the ole C.S.E. thing. Although I hate our school more than I hate any other building.'

'Well, why didn't you stay on?' I cried.

'Because my parents don't think I'm brainy enough,' said Linda. 'They don't think it's worth it. And besides, we're not exactly well off, so I'll be helpful there.'

'If your old man can afford to run a car,' I said, 'then he should think about you and let you stay on for the C.S.E. exam if you want to.'

She smiled. 'Come on, Don. Don't goo on like my owd woman. Le's go back to the pictures to meet me dad.' So I helped her into her coat and we went back to the city centre.

'Can I—can I come out with you again?' I asked her as we waited. She looked up at me sort of dreamily from under half-closed eyes, with her hands in her coat pockets. She shrugged her shoulders. 'Tomorrow too soon?' No answer. 'Nex' Sat'dee then, Linda? I'll meet you at the same place, same time.' She looked out into the lights of the traffic. She looked across the Square at the Town Hall. The big clock struck ten and a few minutes later her old man's green banger pulled into the curb. I put my hand on Linda's arm, practically whispered a good night, and then I went. I walked fast and without looking back and hearing Linda call me back—if she ever did call me back—and I didn't even stop until I came down near to Woolworth's. Then I turned back and caught a bus to Housenal.

Instead of trying to replace the money I had stolen from Mrs. Beharn I had to get more. But I didn't half-inch that. I worked for it round a scrap-yard on Hadley Yard. I worked from the Monday until the Friday afternoon. I didn't see Linda again until the Saturday evening. Again I was frightened that she wouldn't turn up, but I got there and saw her standing in the same place as before. This time I took her hand and spoke the first words quite easily.

'Heyup Lin. How'd it go for you at work?'

'Awful,' she said. 'It teks a bit of gettin' used to, but the people are ever so nice.'

Her face grew into smiles as the night wore on. We enjoyed ourselves in amusement arcades, last house at pictures, the Yankee-bar, where we bought a couple of hot dogs and scoffed them on our way back to meet her dad and his banger. I asked her if we could go for a walk tomorrow if it was fine and she said that'd be nice and asked me to call for her at ten in the morning.

As it turned out the sun was shining for a change the next day. We got the bus to Trowell and walked to the canal and Ilkeston. We turned off the road on to the canal path and walked alongside the canal towards Stanton. Near the iron foundry we came into an uncomfortable and sweaty kiss.

Before we could go on walking past Stanton to get to Stapleford and Stony Clouds, we spotted three of the toughest Ruffnall lads sitting on the lock gates. Their bikes were lying on the grass nearby. Just our luck that we had to bump into *them*! Of all the places they could have gone to in

Nottinghamshire, Derbyshire and Leicestershire, they had to pick Stanton.

I'd planned to take Linda up Stony Clouds, then later to walk to Sandiacre and get a bus back to Nottingham. But now we'd have to pass these three, and I knew there'd be trouble.

We approached the lock gates and they saw us. 'Look, it's Linda Terris and the queer boy.'

'*Oh no*,' Linda groaned, squeezing my hand. 'Let's go back. We've walked far enough.'

'We ain't lettin' them spoil our walk,' I told her.

One of the louts, Sharp, big and thick-set, got off the lock gates and stood in the middle of the path. 'Heyup! Gordon, the bleedin' homosexual. Out for a stroll are you, Gordon? Don't bring your scrubber up here, Gordon.'

Me and Linda stopped. 'Watch your bloody great mouth, Sharp. Because I ain't particularly interested in what you call me but if you call Linda names there'll be trouble.'

'Big talk,' said Sharp.

'There'll be big action if you do,' I warned.

'Homo!' he grinned.

'He can't be a homo if he kicks about wi' Linda,' said Halmish, from the lock gates. 'He's a bisexual. Don't mind a bit of both.'

'Gordon's a ben!' laughed Sharp. 'He's bent beyond straightenin', the bender. Ole Terris 'as got hersen 'ooked up wi' ole bummer boy, 'ere.'

'Don't he look big with the sun shinin' on his leather jacket!' I said to Linda, all sarcastic-like. 'Big and tough. The only trouble is that it i'n't leather. It's cheap plastic.'

'Shut your knowall gob, Gordon,' snapped Sharp. 'You wanna pick a real bit of frock up. Not a scrawny old whore like 'er.'

Have you ever had a time when you've seen nothing but scarlet. And when you somehow get the strength of a maniac because you know you've got to give a good account of yourself? Well, I knew perfectly well that Sharp didn't mean it; he was only getting at *me*. But one thing: nobody says that about Linda to me. And another thing: nobody uses her as a weapon against me because they haven't needed weapons in the past. I'm not kidding you—I swept that boyo off of his smelly feet and we rolled about in the muck thumping sweet merry hell out of each other. His two mates didn't do a thing but watch and cheer Sharp on. Linda watched in silence, knowing that a skinny post like me didn't stand a chance with a brute like Sharp, and I was wondering if it would ever end. It was me that ended it because as we rolled about he got my elbow between the legs. Hard. It was so fast the three spectators couldn't have noticed it. I got up quickly as Sharp rolled about, screaming in pain and yelling, 'You dirty bleeder . . .' On and on he yelled and swore at me. I thumped him in the gob twice more and then I walked back to Linda. Linda took me by my arm and we started walking in the direction we had come from. I tried to walk slow, making out that I wasn't scared with a 'Let 'em come an' bloody-well try it again' attitude, but Linda must have known the truth of it, and she didn't want any more trouble. So she tried to walk faster. She looked over her shoulder. 'Ronnie and Halmish are comin' after us. Come on, Don, run!' 'No,' I said, but she started running, so I ran after her and pretty soon the thugs gave up chase, yelling after us, 'We'll get yo' at school Gordon, you've had it.'

A week later I was back at school and I was even happy on my first day back. I had another date arranged with Linda for Friday night. Could I be more happy? Everything was all right now. I got along with the boys and girls fine. Sharp and the other louts lost interest in the idea of kicking my head in when they started to think I wasn't frightened of them. Even catty-bitchy Marie said 'hello' when we bumped into each other. Friday was soon upon me and I went through the day like a dream. Every lesson was happy; every break time was happy. I had two pounds to take Linda downtown on again. Two quid that I'd earned labouring round the scrap-yard on Monday, Tuesday and Thursday evenings.

That evening we laughed our way through bright lights, music, dancing, drinking and eating—Linda and me. I saw Nottingham like I'd never seen the place before. Never happier before in my life. I could see she was really enjoying it as she creased her face into smiles that made her look very pretty in the coloured lights of the Laughing Hell Discotheque. I kissed her three times. The first was a prattish peck and a flop. But I gave her two beauties before her old man came with the banger to take her home. It had been such a grand evening that we arranged for the next date to be on the following Thursday, and maybe one for the evening after that.

Life was working.

But what happens to you when it stops working?

When you think about it, you know, death can't be bad. And a person who commits suicide is not a coward. It takes courage to turn on the gas tap, swallow the pills, cut your throat, slash your wrists, shoot yourself or hang yourself. It's not a coward's way out. It's a way out for people whose lives have stopped working. People who are disgusted with the world they live in. A world that didn't have to become the way it is now. The rat-race was built by man and if man had wanted to he could have prevented it in the first place. Man could have prevented future wars and people dying of starvation. You know what I mean.

The people who take their lives are people who can't find another world. They can't cut themselves off from the rat-race world to a peaceful world in which everybody is nice and helpful to everbody. There could have been a world like that if man had used his head to start with.

The old people—old people who are crippled—live lonely. Waiting to die. We all must die. We can't avoid it. But I don't want to live through a life of bitterness and then when I'm old have to wait for the day of death, however long it takes to come. But I can't kill myself. I'm not brave enough to throw myself from the roof of a house into Tennon Street; not brave enough to take an overdose of drugs in case I started coughing the tablets up. I'm not brave enough to use a razor-blade or anything sharp on myself. I couldn't face those.

Yet I'll be dead before I'm thirty. Because what I'll do is I'll save up and buy a motor bike. They're pretty useful things to commit suicide on—but it wouldn't really be suicide. I'd just be riding along too fast and too far out into the road. Maybe I'd be speeding down this winding hill through somewhere like Castle Donnington and suddenly I'd crash it and be killed. It would be accidental. I would never know what happened. I wouldn't be waiting for death. It would just happen. A surprise to everyone. And a bit of a shock, maybe, for Linda.

This idea started developing in my mind about a week after that last date with Linda. Thursday came round and I was cracking jokes with some of the lads in the class. Everything was bright. Some of the kids said I was starting to cheer the place up. I had a natural wit, they said. But it all fell to the ground like the rain when Marie came over from her desk to mine and said to me:

'Linda doesn't want ter go out wi' yer anymore. She says don't turn up tonight because she won't be there.'

It had to be. Inside I had been waiting for it to come like an old man waits for death. It had to be. Could never last. Good things never do. I was at school and so I couldn't run away to be on my own. I was a schoolboy and Linda was a working girl.

'Come on, Don,' groaned Main. 'Finish your story then. It's downright inhuman to leave us dangling in mid-air like that . . .' His voice trailed off into nowhere. Quicker than ever before I cut myself off from their world and once again I became the misery of the school, not saying another word for two weeks, and after that only grunting goodbyes and hellos and yes's and no's to people who spoke to me. Once or twice I even found myself crying in the street or in the school playground. All the friends I had suddenly gained at school I lost. They didn't know the reason for my change from misery to happiness and back to misery again. My teacher knew, Marie knew and I knew. But nobody else did. Soon I just ignored people who spoke to me, throwing myself into worse fits of depression behind a wall that they couldn't see and didn't know was there. Because people remind me of my dad, and that's summat I don't ever want to be reminded of.

I hoped that Marie would tell Linda what she had done to me and hoped that it would hurt her. But then I thought, no, that's unfair. Why should I wish ill on the only person I ever cared about? So instead I wished her well and good luck from where I was to wherever she was.

All my dreams of Linda
Have been burnt to a cinder.
I'm dead in her mind
Yet she's lovely and kind.

As Don looked across at Tommy, still deep in his newspaper, he rememberd what Ronald Harrison had said to him: 'You know, Don, if you could care for Linda that much, you could care for someone else too. When you were happy with Linda, you smartened yourself up, you were nice to people, and you found they were nice to you. Well, lad, just *try* to keep it up—even though you feel empty and miserable inside. That way, you'll meet someone else. That way you'll be happy again.'

But Don had tried to put this into practice before, though he hadn't thought it out in so many words. Ron Harrison's advice was good; he'd just tried to make it work with the wrong people. It was through making this sort of effort that he'd managed to go around with Jamie Howe and Bob Denham. He hadn't wanted to get mixed up in the fruit machine game, but it had sort of happened—when they'd had a right merry evening on the town. As for Val Harpe and her old man's forty-eight nicker, she'd only had to open her big brown eyes at him, and promise him *anything*, to have him pinching the lolly while she kept Jamie occupied. What a bitch that girl had been! Planting it in Jamie's saddle-bag and then telling so many lies to the magistrate that everyone felt sorry for such a sweet, young innocent girl—getting mixed up with a couple of crooked thugs like himself and Jamie Howe.

The juke box was silent and Trev, Sheila and the crowd at the next table got up to go, all talking at once.

'Terrar. Wouldn't be in your shoes, Don!' said Sheila as

she passed.

Tommy put down his newspaper and was looking hard at Don.

'Now come on, mate,' he said. 'Tell us all about it. What's this Jamie 'Owe got on you?'

'All right then. If I don't tell yer, everybody else will. Let's 'ave some more tea, an' I'll tell yer.'

FIVE

Jamie walked down Tennon Street towards Hadley Yard at half-past seven on Monday morning. He was due to start work at Knight and Drew's pencil factory at eight o'clock, and Wilf had made sure he was up and out in good time. Hadley Yard was where all the factories were, and at that time in the morning Tennon Street was crowded with workers arriving. Some walked, some came by bicycle, scooter or car. Jamie joined the procession on the pavement, hating the guts of everyone he saw. 'Curris an' 'is bleedin' job!' he mumbled.

He had to pass his old school, a grim, ugly building, on the other side of the road. The entrance was a gate under the main arch on which were the words:

THE JAMES RUFFNALL SCHOOL
1853-1935

He remembered that this was the first day of the September term, and that in a little while Tennon Street would once again be invaded by children between the ages of eleven and sixteen tearing up it on bicycles, spitting in the gutters, shooting phlegm at each other, lighting up cigarettes, boys yelling after girls, girls yelling back at boys and everybody swearing.

His own weapon against teachers who pushed him around had always been a note to the headmaster reading: 'Dear

Mr. Brentwood, Please excuse our Jamie from homework as it is keeping him up too late.' Brentwood had written back explaining that each pupil was only set an hour's work and he couldn't possibly see how it could be keeping Jamie up so late. But Jamie had enjoyed telling teachers that he wasn't doing homework and they couldn't make him. When they demanded why, he used to display his cocky grin and say, 'Yer c'n ask Mr. Brentwood if yer don't believe me'. Some teachers left it at that but others got shirty, then he'd tell them, "Tain't my fault, sir. See me mam about it, not me.'

Jamie had been the king show-off of Ruffnall. He had to be liked, had to be admired—by his friends, enemies and strangers. Being the hero, to Jamie, was to throw his weight around showing the girls what muscles he had; it also meant a fag between his lips and a good-looking bike with drop handlebars to ride about on for all to stand agog as he sped around on his ten-speed racer.

He remembered his first morning as a fourth year. Him and Bob Denham had rambled into the yard, top dogs, about to prove that they were in charge of things. They stood at the girls' arch, cheeking the girls off as they went through into their own yard. Standing with them was Bob's girl, Lynn.

The first new girls walked nervously towards them. Bob watched them and wolf-whistled. He pushed his way into the group and brought out an eleven-year-old girl with a boy's haircut, National Health glasses and red socks right up to her knees. Her friends didn't hang about. They vanished into the girls' yard.

The girl went white as Bob looked her up and down. He let out a howl of laughter and pointed at her socks. He looked at Jamie and Lynn. 'Jeezie Christ,' he screamed, 'look at them *bleddy* socks! 'Ave yer *ever* seen owt *like* 'em? I say!' He kept on walking round her doing a belly dance.

'Ooh-la-la!'

'Boggerin' ada,' Jamie said, sauntering up to the girl with his hands in his pockets. 'Heyup, lirrle girl. Them're raspers, ent thee? Yo' gonner play football in them socks?'

'Nor,' stammered the girl.

'Nor?' said Bob, ceasing his belly dance.

'Nor,' Jamie told Bob. 'Ah think wiv gort a bit orv a Scortch bint on our hands, Angus.'

'Is that sor?' said Bob. 'Is that sor, Aggie? Der yer nae mean a *wee* Scortch bint, Aggie?'

'Do Ah mean a *wee* Scortch bint?' Jamie asked the girl. He turned back to Bob. 'Ah thing Ah *do* Angus!'

The girl spoke up bravely, 'Ah'm from Halifax, York-shire.'

Lynn came to the girl's rescue, and pushed her through the archway to the girls' playground.

By now Jamie had reached Hadley Yard and joined the stream of men going down it.

They didn't really change me at Kellowyn, he told himself again. The only thing they changed about me was my attitude towards people. I couldn't give a sweet hairy sod who likes me or not now. As long as I like mesen and Julie likes me and I can take care of number one, then what the 'ell? The lads at Kellowyn joined my gang because they knew that Dion Kilgrady had liked me and everybody liked Dion Kilgrady. I got all them mates without effort. Most of them snivellin' youths that were born thieves.

The world's cruel, but what meks it cruel yer've got to ask yourself? It ain't the birds an' the bees, the dogs an' the cats, the cows an' the goats and you can't blame God, either. Because He put the first tribe of humans down here and when He saw what rotten sods they were He left them to it.

Jamie turned in at the gates of the pencil factory, stuck his hands in his pockets and pushed his way through to where they were clocking in.

The following Saturday, Jamie woke up early. He had gone easy on the drink the night before, at The Green Leaves. With one hand holding a glass of brown ale and the other holding Julie's, it had been a fair night.

He got himself a quick breakfast and then, at ten past nine, sat at the table smoking a fag. He wondered what Dion Kilgrady's partner would be like. He imagined a rugged-looking youth, a bit on the squatty side. If he knew Adam Clint, as Kilgrady had told him, it could be interesting—not that Jamie had ever heard of Adam Clint, but from the way Kilgrady had gone on about him he sounded quite big. Jamie had kept his eyes open for the name in the *Nottingham Evening Post* all week but nothing had been reported.

At ten to eleven Jamie climbed the steps to the flat Kilgrady had told him to come to. There was a label on the door on which was written:

D. KILFARREN
C. CHATTERNY

He knocked. Nobody came. He knocked three times and the door was eventually opened by Kilgrady, wearing a red silk dressing-gown over pyjamas. His thick black hair was tangled, his eyes looked sore, he needed a shave and he blinked as he looked out at Jamie. Jamie said:

'My Christ, you look like yer've bin shot in the 'ead.'

'Oh, it's you,' groaned Kilgrady.

'Are you ready for me, or is that too stupid a question? It was you who said eleven o'clock Sat'dee mornin', yer know.'

'Jaysus, was ut?' groaned Kilgrady, scratching the side of his head. 'C'mon in.' He led him into an expensively-furnished flat.

Kilgrady pulled the curtains in the living room, clutching his head again as he let in the light.

'Hey,' said Jamie, looking around him. 'This is quite a place, i'n't it!'

'You don't expect a hard-workin' lad like meself to live in a pigsty, do ya?'

'Ey a rough night?'

'You can see for yourself. Sure, I've only just gone to bed, let alone time to get up!'

'At least you slept in a bed, not wi' the bleedin' fairies like I 'ad ter!'

'Ah—so you did,' said Kilgrady, suddenly coming to life. 'What about my fiver?'

Jamie handed him two pound notes. 'I'll 'ave to finish payin' you off next week, the week after an' the week after that if you don't mind, thanks, Dee.'

'Well, did you see the girl?'

'Yeh. Me an' Julie are all patched up now. Took her to the Odeon on Wednesday and The Green Leaves on Tennon Street last night. An' if I 'ave my wonderful way it'll not end there, either. She's great.'

'Sure, she is. So that's how things are, eh?' said Kilgrady, putting the two pound notes in his dressing-gown pocket.

'Yeh, that's how things are,' said Jamie.

'Ah well,' said Jamie, 'where's your mate? C. Chatterny. Charlie Chatterny?'

'Here, young man,' said a voice from behind. Jamie turned and saw a middle-aged, grey-haired man with a lined face, standing in the doorway of the kitchen. He tied his dressing-gown cord tighter and walked across the room to shake Jamie's hand. 'Charles Chatterny.'

'Heyup, mate. I'm Jamie Howe.'

'Dion's told me about you,' said Mr. Chatterny. 'Sit down here at the table where I can see you.'

The table was a round, polished one, standing in the recess of a window that looked on to a large garden. Kilgrady went to the bathroom. Chatterny and Jamie looked at each other.

'Dion tells me he met you at Kellowyn Court,' Chatterny said with a slight note of sarcasm. 'The place where they put the naughty boys from over Tennon Street way.'

Jamie needled. 'Not only Tennon-Streeters. Dion got bundled off there for knocking off bottles of whiskey in Long Eaton. Only ponces call 'em naughty boys' places. Most people call us yobs or thugs or summat. Juvenile delinquents.'

'Hm, but Dion tells me you were innocent of the crimes they put you away for,' said Chatterny.

'I was innocent of one of the crimes I was charged with and innocent of one of the accusations. A lad planted some loot on my bike what he'd nicked out of this bird's 'ouse. Then the scuffers got me for stickin' up the fruities on New Tennon Street. I did that, all right. I got hauled off ter Tennon Street cophouse and ended up gettin' charged wi' thievin' forty-eight quid and them tryin' ter mek me admit I raped this sixteen-year-old girl. I admit I'm as crooked as a zig-zag but I never touched a penny, a button or a zip that had owt ter do wi' Val Harpe. She should be so lucky! You don't think I'm a member of the criminal set? Well I am, mate. Rearing ter goo. Just waitin' for a chance ter get serrup in business.'

'Dion said you had the right ideas,' said Chatterny, 'but you need more than that. Thieves are thieves for the money they think they can get. Big jobs need a lot of hard thinking and hard planning. A lot of knowledge and experience goes into the planning. It isn't just a matter of waltzing into a bank and helping yourself to the cash, you know.'

'What *is* it a matter of, then?'

Chatterny looked him coldly in the eye and said, 'Good thieves stay on the right side of the institution gates.'

'Ah,' said Jamie. 'Except when they're framed in gold like the bleedin' Mona Lisa.'

'You've got a job, haven't you? Where's that?'

'Knight and Drew's pencil factory. They're puttin' me through the trainin' stage. I've 'ad a week there, an' the sooner I can gerrout for good, the better I'll like it. I want to earn some real money—live in comfort, wear posh clothes. That'll mek my old man look silly. Dion an' me was mates in Borstal. Wot 'e can do, I can do too.'

'You're doing at least one honest job,' said Chatterny. 'Stick to that till you know how clever you are.'

'Well? Are yer goin' ter give me a chance?'

Chatterny looked out of the window for a few seconds. 'I'll tell you what, son. If you come back at ten-thirty to-night, with a hundred pounds which you've stolen yourself, we'll think about it a little more.'

'*A hundred what?*' exclaimed Jamie.

'That's the test, sonny,' said Chatterny. 'A hundred! And no bright ideas about going to the police about me and Dion if you don't get the money or get caught trying to take it. Because I have friends that take care of . . .'

'Don't! Don't get nasty wi' me, mate,' said Jamie, walking

89

to the door. ''Cos if I send you ter chokeyland ah'll mek bleddy sure you're followed swiftly by Adam Clint an' 'is merrie men.' Jamie slammed the door shut behind him.

The time had come. Time to get out and steal. But how? And where? Jamie felt nervous about it. He kept telling himself it was the easiest thing in the world to do, unless he'd turned yellow. But after that he'd say to himself: What if I'm caught? I'll go back to Curris again—for a much longer time than last.

The day went by surprisingly fast and at half-past nine Jamie kicked a tin can down a dark road that had only one street light in it. When he came to the lamp-post he looked up at the house behind it. It was a house he knew. The man who owned it was certainly well-off. He remembered the house in every detail. It was all in darkness. The next-door neighbour's bathroom light came on and shone light across to one of the side windows. The window was open an inch or two at the top. But there was no drain pipe near or any easy way of getting up to it. He cursed.

At just gone half-past ten Jamie knocked on the door of Kilgrady and Chatterny's flat. Kilgrady swung it open to him. He was dressed up right loud and flashy in a red silk shirt and gold cuff-links. Jamie pushed past him into the room crying excitedly, 'I've gorrit, I've gorrit. Every penny on it . . . an' more, I bet . . .' He stopped, seeing two teenage girls sitting on the settee. One was Dolly Benson and the other was a flashy-looking fairy dressed in this silver kind of mini-dress and she had quite long legs. Christ, thought Jamie.

'He's in the bedroom, there. Go on in,' Kilgrady told him.

'Ah, right-o,' said Jamie. He nodded at Dolly. 'Heyup, luv.'

He crossed the room to the bedroom door, knocked and went straight into an elaborate-looking bedroom and closed the door. Chatterny was sitting on the edge of the large double bed tying a rose-pink tie to go with his smart suit.

'Hello,' said Jamie. 'Yo' an' Dion sleep together in one bed? Kinky!'

'Look, son, you'll have to grow up, won't you? You've got a lot to learn. Where's the hundred pounds?' said Chatterny. 'Did you get it?'

'Yeh,' said Jamie. 'But I could 'ave borrowed it for all you'd know. You should o' told me to go and swipe jewels or summat, shouldn't you!' He pulled out rolls of fivers and dropped them on the bed. From his coat pockets he pulled out small boxes and cases and dropped those on the bed too. Together they opened the boxes and cases to find brooches, ear-rings, necklaces, bracelets and rings. Chatterny counted the money.

'Fifty-five pounds in fivers,' said Chatterny. 'At least that in jewels—some are worthless, but some are real.'

'Clever, eh?' grinned Jamie happily.

'Where did you get it all?'

Jamie laughed. 'You'll never guess. I really did do that bird's place tonight—old Harpe. You know—"Harpe's Enterprizes". I thought ter mesen, I wonder if that twit still leaves his cash lyin' about? So I took this ladder out of his shed in the garden and climbed through an upstairs window. There was nobody in. I found this chest-like box in the bedroom. About—what?—say, fifteen inches long, twelve inches high and nine wide. Heavy as an elephant. Well, it makes me laugh when on telly you get some secret agent bloke after documents and when they break into these places to nick the documents they 'ang about reading them, just begging for someone to come along and nab them. Well, I didn't stand about trying to open this little chest. I lobbed it out the window, climbed down the ladder and then chucked the ladder in the long grass. The chest was bust open but nowt had fallen out. I closed it up and took me mac off and wrapped it around this chest and then I nipped along to the nearest pub where I went into the bogs and stuffed all the chest's contents into my pockets. Then I rushed to the bus station, near the hospitals. I got on a Trent bus bound for Derby—the opposite way from my home. It had ten minutes before take-off. So I planted the chest on the back seat—no one saw me—then I slipped off and came straight here. That bus'll be on its way through Wollaton to Bramcote by now. All right, get your mitts off. Have I proved mesen?'

'Not bad, for a first job. But don't get too cocky,' said Chatterny. 'Better leave this stuff here until Monday. I'll get a friend of mine to value it. Then we'll hide it until it's cool and flog it later.'

'Ah, well I ain't so sure,' said Jamie, standing up.

'You ain't so sure? Look, son, you do as I say around here, or forget about coming in with us. I give the orders, you carry 'em out. Understand?'

'O.K.,' said Jamie, stuffing the money in his pockets. 'I just don't want anything to happen to it, though, Mr. Chatterny. I'll tek this brooch for me girl-friend.'

Chatterny grunted and Jamie pocketed the brooch.

'When's our first job together?' asked Jamie.

'We'll talk about it if you call at seven o'clock, Monday evening,' said Chatterny.

'Right,' Jamie grinned and added. 'If one o' them scrubbers out there is yourn you'd berrer get there quick because Dion'll be teachin' 'er the facts of life by now.'

'He doesn't need to teach them a thing,' Chatterny told

92

him. 'They'll be teaching *him*.'

But that wasn't how Jamie saw it as he crossed the living room to leave. Kilgrady was swinging the girl with long legs and the silver mini-dress across his stomach with their lips locked together, on the settee. Dolly was pouring herself a drink at the bar. It would be her turn in a few moments.

Jamie closed the door behind him.

By mid-October three successful raids on shops had been carried out by Jamie, Kilgrady, and Chatterny. Chatterny always stayed at home and planned the job in detail. Kilgrady would give him all the relevant information about a place and a plan of the shop they would be breaking into; Chatterny worked it out from there. He hardly ever seemed to go out and Jamie believed that his main use was in the high-up friends he had—friends who could help get rid of some of the hot stuff in a hurry, or get *them* out of the area in a hurry if the cops got too close for comfort. Jamie was irritated because Kilgrady and he did all the dirty work, yet Chatterny managed to store the loot somewhere else. Kilgrady said Chatterny had it in a house in Wollaton but he wouldn't give either of them the address. Chatterny told them that the loot must stay put for a while until the police weren't on the alert for it. You couldn't be too careful.

Jamie couldn't make out the relationship between Kilgrady and Chatterny. Kilgrady seemed to have known the older man for a very long time and always took notice of what he said. Chatterny sometimes spoke roughly to Kilgrady, but usually he was possessive, cajoling, and became worried if the boy was away a long time. Yet Jamie sensed that something was wrong. He didn't know what, but it seemed as if Kilgrady and Chatterny didn't trust each other.

One day Kilgrady confessed some of his anxieties to Jamie. He knew that Adam Clint was still at the Carnden Hotel and that six more of his men had just come down from Manchester. He wasn't sure of Chatterny's connection with Clint, but it disturbed him. He had been uneasy about it for some time, so he always carried a gun. Somehow the police had got to know about this gun and were after him for it. Kilgrady felt the time was coming when he would do better working on his own, or with only Jamie to help. He could dispose of the loot himself, and he would have more freedom. But Kilgrady looked worried; leaving Chatterny wasn't as easy as it might seem.

'Why?' asked Jamie.

'Well,' said Kilgrady, 'I owe him quite a lot. He was the only one who looked after me—in his way—when my old man died. You see—he's my uncle. My mother's brother.'

'Yer uncle!' exclaimed Jamie. 'Christ! Why didn't yer tell me?'

'Sure, it didn't seem to matter. We had more important things to think about.'

Jamie was thinking now. Hard. Charles Chatterny might be wanted by the police for robbery, but if they were to catch up with him, Chatterny would be in trouble—trouble more serious than robbery.

Jamie was by now trusted by his father. Wilf had heard that his son was doing well at the factory, and certainly he never failed to pay up the three pounds rent on time. Jamie knew that his father was beginning to change. He was relaxing more and smiling more. Not as sharp as he used to be. Soon he could see him and his dad getting on together like they'd never done before. Pity he's left it so late to get like this, he thought. Pity he couldn't have given some help when it was needed. But if that's how things are, then I'll soon have a bloody good laugh at the way I'm kidding him and everyone else in Tennon Street.

They sat at the table eating breakfast one Thursday morning before work. Wilf was reading the paper and Dot was in the scullery. The radio's battery was dead. All was silent as Jamie sat thinking about his job at Knight and Drew's. It was a good cover for him, he thought. Although he seemed to slog his guts out in the factory the cash came in handy at the end of the week. Soon he would be getting his cut from the loot which was, Chatterny had told him, gradually leaving the Wollaton house.

He put his knife and fork down and asked his father if there was anything in the paper. Wilf told him that there was just the same as usual: strikes, murders, robberies and half-naked girls . . .

'Sounds interestin',' beamed Jamie. 'I'll have ter read it after you then. Paper lad was early this mornin' wa'n't 'e?'

Wilf said that it was a new one—a girl this time. More alive and careful. Earlier than the lad too. Wilf reckoned that paper *girls* were better and he guessed that Ted Brown had gone up Bilco's and got the lad sacked. Wilf folded his paper and put it down on the table.

'I'm glad ye'r settlin' down to a good job, lad. Like a sensible adult.'

'I told you before,' said Jamie. 'I was just a kid doin' summat for excitement. Just had ter slip up an' tek what wa' comin'. I'd 'ave thought you'd 'ave been able to understand that. I'm straight. I ain't even seen Bob Denham or any of the others since I've been back. Anyway, I'm off to work now. See you tonight. Can I tek the paper?'

'Ah,' said Wilf. 'The *Evening Post*'s under the telly on the trolly if you want it. See yer, then.'

At one o'clock Jamie knocked off for dinner break. He un-wrapped his sandwiches, poured some tea from his flask and turned to the *Nottingham Evening Post*. He nearly fell over backwards when he opened the first page and found Charlie Chatterny's face staring at him under the headline:

'MARRY-ME' MURDERER IN NOTTS
Keft seen in Wollaton

Underneath the photograph were the words: *Ernest Keft, wanted for two murders and attempted murder.*

Jamie read the passage three times before believing it.

Ernest Keft, known as the 'Marry-me' murderer, is believed to be staying in Wollaton. Reports have been received from people who claim to have seen him there.

Keft, 52, is wanted in connection with the murders of Gillian Harvey, 1962, Jacqueline Vaughan, 1962, and the attempt on the life of a nineteen-year-old girl, 1966. All three crimes were committed in Kent.

Police warn that he may be dangerous and should not be approached by members of the public.

Jamie could hardly believe it. Old Chatterny! A killer? A woman killer? Well, Christ, he must be a psycho, Jamie said to himself. Wonder if Dion knows? Blimey, I bet he does an' all. No wonder Dion's been so worried. No wonder he wants to get away!

That afternoon Jamie's mind wasn't on his job. The more he thought about that newspaper report, the more carried away he became by an idea. He needed more money; his cut from the jobs they'd done wasn't coming quick enough. Blackmail was something new. It was something to be thought about—carefully.

He wasn't giving his job full concentration and the foreman noticed.

'Summat up lad?' the foreman asked.

'Yeh!'

'What?'

'This little factory.'

'What's up wi' factory?'

'A couple of barrels of TNT, if I had me way,' Jamie laughed and carried on with his work.

Friday went along the same. Jamie not paying enough attention to his job, thinking and thinking about all the money he could squeeze out of Charlie Chatterny. It would be a tricky thing, but well worth trying.

And at six o'clock Jamie stepped off Tennon Street into a telephone kiosk, outside the public library. He dialled Kilgrady's number and stubbed out his fag on the wall. When he spoke he tried to change his accent into what he thought sounded Scottish.

'Hello,' the voice at the other end of the line grunted. It was Chatterny.

'May Ah speak tae a Mr. Ernest Keft?' Jamie asked. He felt silly. His Scottish accent didn't sound too Scottish after all.

'Who?'

'Och, come on Mr. Keft,' said Jamie. 'Why use such a silly name as Charlie Chatterny? It sounds more like an old time comedian. Especially when you're so well known as Mr. Keft. Mr. *Ernest* Keft. The murderer.'

'Who is this?' the urgent voice cried.

'Me name's Benny,' said Jamie. 'Ah'm a blackmailer.' There was silence for a few seconds. 'I'll not call ye Mr. Keft. I'll call you Ernest. Right? Fine.'

'Get off the line!'

'Why? Have ye not had time to hang your washin' oot, lately, Ern? Before I ring off I must tell you that ye'd better take to Fugitive Highway if ye don't do as I say. Because I know where y'are and I'll be watching ye round the clock, matey-o.'

'What do you want?' Keft asked.

'That's better,' said Jamie. 'Ye're goin' to be very charitable this week-end, Ern. You're goin' to deposit a hundred pounds in the collection box in the church on the corner of Sindeman Street. St. Matthew's. It wouldn'a be wise o'ye to bring company of any sort. No gangsters, no police. And don't wait about for me. After ye've deposited the money in the collection box, go home. Or else there'll be trouble. The money must be there by quarter to twelve tomorrow night. Bye for now.' Jamie rang off and mopped his brow with his handkerchief. He stepped back on to the street. The rain was falling heavily so he pulled up his collar and started walking towards the bus stop.

Next morning Jamie paid his usual Saturday visit to Kilgrady and Keft. The door wasn't locked so he walked straight in, but stood still in the hallway as he heard loud voices coming from the living room. He listened. Kilgrady was shouting: '. . . an' I been doin' a lot o' thinkin' myself, lately. You know what I've been thinkin'? I said to meself the other day, Dion, what's it worth? You've had a good run in this town. Isn't now the time to get out while there's still a chance? You're gettin' to be hot stuff an' the cops can put you away for a long time over that Darker revolver. Nottingham's no use to you any more. You stay an' you could become as neurotic as your Uncle Ernest. What's it worth with the Notts. police after you, Adam Clint an' his mob in town and a very wanted man for your uncle who's been by your side since the old man died, an' since after you left Kellowyn? When I get all my money from the house in Wollaton I'm goin' home ter Galway. It'll be soon now. I'm leavin' Nottingham an' I'm leavin' England. But I'm leavin' *you*!'

'That's enough, Dion,' said Keft angrily. 'You've gone mad. You *won't* leave here. You'll stay right where you are. You've just got into a panic because I told you I'm being blackmailed, but blackmailers can be shut up just like anyone else can . . .'

At this point Jamie tapped loudly on the door and walked in. 'Heyup, Dee. Charlie.'

All three looked at each other in silence, then Keft spoke.

'What the hell do you mean walking straight in like that? How long were you out there?'

'Long enough to hear the word "blackmail" as I came in,' said Jamie, with a false worried expression on his face. 'I bet all your neighbours know about it too, you was speakin' so loud. What's goin' on? Some sneak up Wollaton found out about us three or summat? Only I can't afford ter be the next to be blackmailed, can I?'

'Oh, an' you think I can afford to be the first?' cried Keft.

'Yeh,' snapped Jamie. 'I do, mate. For a start you've got more loot in that Wollaton house than I can think of.'

'That belongs to all three of us,' said Kilgrady.

'Aye, an' it worries me,' said Jamie. 'You see, I don't know where this house is. If owt happens to *him* I've risked mesen for sweet nothin'. An' I bet if *he's* gettin' blackmailed, then me an' yo' are on the list. How much does 'e want?'

'A hundred,' said Keft.

'*What*?' cried Jamie. 'I a'n't got that. For when?'

'Tonight,' said Keft. 'A chap called Benny, with a faked Scots accent, rang me last night.'

'Christ, 'e 'ardly gis yer a chance ter fart, does 'e? said Jamie, trying to look even more worried.

'I bet the bloke won't lay off, either,' said Kilgrady. 'Once the sons of vermin get a hold on you that's it. With their hands around your neck they squeeze an' squeeze an' squeeze, uppin' the price for silence all the time. When there's nuttin' left to squeeze out of you you'll find yourself arrested by the cops. Booked good an' proper.'

'Where are yer gonner get the money from if you ain't got it now?' Jamie wanted to know.

Keft stared out of the window. 'Ha! Where? is right. You tell me.'

'What are you gonna do? Knock over Barclay's?' joked Jamie.

'We can't knock over a fruit stall at the market,' said Keft. 'The police will be workin' out our moves now. If Dion makes too many unnecessary trips out of here they'll pick him up for that gun. No, the best help I can get is Adam Clint. I worked for him in London. He'll help me.'

'Tuh,' said Kilgrady, rolling his eyes upwards.

'He's here in Nottingham lying low for a while,' said Keft. 'Taking a breather. I'll go and have a chat with him. See if I can borrow the cash.'

'Well,' smiled Jamie. 'I seem to be the only one life is running smoothly for. What wi' Dion an' the pop-gun, yo' and the blackmailer, and Clint the gangster king still hanging about . . . Still, luck has been owed ter me for a long time.'

'Luck indeed!' grunted Kilgrady. 'Will you ever run out of it, for Jaysus sake? A day or two out of Kellowyn and what's he got? Love an' money.'

'I've been livin' on Badluck Street all my life,' said Jamie.

'Now I've moved on to Goodluck Street. Thanks to my mate God.'

'Be careful,' Kilgrady warned. 'The council might want to build a supermarket on Goodluck Street and they'll have to knock it down first.'

'Lerrem try,' said Jamie. 'Anyroad, we can't plan anything for a bit—but let me know what 'appens.'

He left.

The next day Julie was preparing Sunday roast dinner when the door-bell rang. She came out of the kitchenette and went to the door. It was Jamie. 'Sorry I'm late, Julie,' he said. 'Aye, but it smells good.'

'Heyup, duck,' she smiled gaily. 'You're not late at all—come and sit down. Dinner won't be ready for another half hour.'

Jamie pulled out a couple of fivers and gave them to her. ''Ere, buy yourself somethin' nice wi' this—a new dress or somethin'.' For a few seconds she stared at them in amazement. Then, 'Blimey, since when have you had money like this to hand out?'

'Didn't yer know?' he said. 'Although we live in a rough old area my old man is pretty successful in life. He owns Howe's Enterprizes.'

'Come on,' she said. 'Don't make me laugh.'

'On my life,' he said, raising his right hand. It took him a little while to convince her that Howe's Enterprizes really did exist, and really was owned by his old man but in the end she believed him. She asked herself why he hadn't told her before and why he never dressed in good-quality clothes, but then she remembered he liked being a rebel and he probably considered wearing rough clothes the way the social rebel went about. She believed him. How could she do otherwise?

Julie liked Jamie for his cheek, his aggressive attitude towards life. He had become the new hero-type of her stories—the romantic Heyward Vandine she had created. Although he had a grudge against the world, he seemed to try and hide his bitterness from her. This 'Howe's Enterprizes' explained the expensive brooch that Jamie had presented her with about a month ago. It also explained how he was able to spend a fair amount on her when he took her out.

But Jamie had won Julie's heart completely when he had taken her tattered novel home and had spent some time reading it, trying to understand everything about it. He'd come back to her a couple of days later, all excited. He told her he couldn't understand why it had been rejected so many times. The novel had depth, the characters were *real* if you bothered to analyse them and get right down to them. That's what he had set himself to do when he had sat down and started on page one, chapter one, and he had done it.

Jamie had come back again and again to talk about the book. Over an evening meal—Julie was taking more care with her cooking these days—they had discussed the backgrounds of the characters, the backgrounds which she had not included in the novel. Through this Jamie and Julie had come closer to each other. They had got excited about each other's ideas. Jamie talked a lot about Tennon Street and some of the rough people he'd known. He was an authority on the subject of teenage social rebels and Julie was a fascinated listener. In each other they had found an understanding. A new kind of friendship and maybe a new kind of love.

Julie liked Jamie too much to disbelieve him.

Monday came and Jamie returned to the telephone kiosk

to phone Keft again. He decided to keep to the phoney Scottish accent. 'Hello Ernest. Benny here. Thanks for getting your wee offering to the St. Matthew's collection box in time. The trouble is, Ernie, Ah need some more cash. Hard times an' a' that. Tax an' everythin' gettin' me doon. Well, everybody's after cash, aren't thee, Ern? I'm afraid it'll need te be a hundred an' fifty this time, sunshine. Ah'm terribly sorry aboot it. Make it for Wednesday—same time, same place. I'm not keepin' you up too late, am Ah?'

'But I can't get that much,' cried Keft. 'I had to borrow that hundred off a friend of mine.'

'Well, I shouldn'a need te tell ye what te do. Knock off a rich man's daughter,' Jamie advised and rang off.

When Jamie called round at the flat later to see how things were, Keft had some news for him. He told him that the blackmailer had called again but this time Clint was going to send one of his men to the church on Sindeman Street. It would be one of Clint's knockeroffers and when Clint's boys hit, they hit hard, quick, sharp and clean.

'So *you* won't need to pay up any blackmail money, son. Nor will anyone else,' Keft said.

'Good,' said Jamie. 'I'm glad. That's a ton weight off me mind.'

He left hurriedly. Won't Clint be pleased when his killer gets back with the news that nobody showed up at St. Matthew's, Sindeman Street, he thought.

SIX

Don Gordon got up early every morning and was one of the first to clock in at Harrington's Ink Factory where he worked. In this way he missed the crowds. He also missed Jamie Howe, who worked in Hadley Yard too. In the evening there were so many people streaming out of the factories at five o'clock that there wasn't much chance of running into Jamie—though it was always a nasty thought in Don's mind.

Since the day he'd told Tommy about Jamie and the Harpe affair, he had shut himself off from everyone. He could be in a room full of people and still not see them, he'd be so deep in thought or depression. He couldn't even talk to Tommy, but Tommy wasn't making things better by lying in bed most of the day and not going to work. The weeks had gone by and Tommy's big ideas about the job he was always going to get had come to nothing. Tommy had had some money to begin with, but now he was always hard up. Even worse, Tommy wasn't paying his share of the rent. Don was paying most of their living expenses these days. He could see the iron bars around Tommy before long.

Don's main ambition was to buy off *all* the motor bike and get out because he'd had enough of Tennon Street and all that it meant. Escaping from his mother had been the first, and so far the last, big step he'd made. Now he must make another one. But how?

On the Wednesday in the third week of November Don came out of Harrington's Ink Factory a few minutes later than the usual five o'clock scramble and walked straight into Jamie Howe. Jamie was standing outside the gates of Knight and Drew's with Gerard Hopker, another man and two girls. Don knew the girls. Carole and Cathy. They were two of those who had made fun of him at school. He knew this would mean trouble. He looked the other way and walked on. He didn't cross the road because they would have known he was trying to avoid them. There was a chance he could pass unnoticed.

But Cathy saw him. She grinned, gave Carole a dig with her elbow and spoke loudly:

'Oh, there's that *boy*.'

'Oh, that *lovely* boy!' sneered Carole.

'Ooh, Ah feel all faint!'

Don carried on walking, but Cathy darted round in front of him and forced him to stop. She had an unlit cigarette between her lips.

'Gor a light, Donald, luv?' she asked.

'That's not my name,' he spoke down his nose at her.

'Wor is it then? What's Don short for if it ain't Donald?'

'Why don't you get lost?' said Don.

'What kind of talk is that to a lady?'

Jamie strode forward and stood facing Don. He said, 'You want to expect it from 'im, Cath! 'E's pig-ignorant. En't yer, Donovan?'

''E's a proper misery guts, i'n't 'e!' said Carole.

'I leave people be,' Don answered. 'You want ter try doin' the same yersen sometime.'

'Don't harm anybody, do yer, Gordon?' said Jamie. Then he looked at the others and shouted, '*This* odd-boy was the

105

gett that got me sent down when I 'adn't done owt. I got two years for summat *'e* did!'

'Don't tell bleddy lies,' snapped Don.

Jamie stared back at him, his eyes blazing with fury.

'*You're* the bleddy liar! You never stopped bleddy lyin'. You can look everybody in the eye but me, tell a lie an' gerraway wi' it. You lied to the Law and you 'ad me sink for summat I didn't do. You're as low as filth! You're a bleedin' sewer rat—and I'm gonna see you crawl back into the slime you crawled out of.'

'Did 'e really do that?' asked Carole.

'What a sod,' said Cathy.

'Drop dead, Howe,' Don spoke between his teeth. '*You're* the liar. If it wasn't for you I would never 'a' bin in trouble wi' the Law in the first place. And I didn't plant that money on you. I've told you it was Val Harpe—she fixed it all!'

'You lyin' bastard,' Jamie yelled, moving closer with clenched fists. Don took a step back. He didn't want to fight Jamie. He knew he couldn't win. Everything seemed to be spinning round him, but he somehow found words: 'You were already on probation. You were allus in trouble when you was a school kid. Everybody knew what a thief you were. I know, 'cos I went around wi' yer. Only I wasn't as good at it as you. You thought you was big an' you told everyone so an' all. You showed off an' you'll never stop showin' off. You're a right *slob*!' Don turned to go. Jamie grabbed his arm and jerked him forward.

'Right! Yer've talked yersen into your own funeral!'

Jamie swung back at him, grabbed him by the lapels and pinned him up against the wall.

'Tryin' ter get yerself back into Borstal, are yer?' gasped Don.

'Be a pleasure as long as I can finish you off first.'

Jamie's fist shot into Don's stomach. Don winced and bowed his head. He looked up at Jamie, glassy-eyed. Suddenly he struggled from Jamie's left hand gripping his collar. He struck out at Jamie's chin. The blow sent Jamie back a few steps. He stepped forward again and knocked Don back against the wall and punched again. Don doubled up, his face twisted with pain. As Jamie was about to let fly another volley of punches, he was grabbed from behind by a thick burly man—one of the crowd that had gathered.

'Hey, pack tharrin, mate,' said the man. 'Want someone to call a copper?'

Jamie tried to free himself and rush at Don again, but he was held by too many hands. Everybody began shouting at once, but he yelled above the noise:

'Yeh! A copper! That's what 'e's 'opin' for. That's all 'e needs. A bleedin' flatfoot to come an' rescue 'im. 'E could never fight owt out for 'issen, the big bleddy *girl*!'

The men dragged Jamie off. Carole and Cathy had disappeared in the thick of the fight. Don was standing upright again, dazed and unseeing.

'Yo' all right, mate?' someone asked him.

'Yeh, Ah'm all right,' he said.

Don steadied himself against the wall, then started to move away. The groups of people were breaking up, and he mingled with them unnoticed as they walked out of Hadley Yard. He wanted to go away and cry somewhere, to be alone, to stop the aching of his mind and body. But where? Not to his mother's. Not to the room he shared with Tommy. Then through the mist of his mind, he remembered Tommy had said he'd be out. He was going after a job and wouldn't be back till later. Don lurched forwards, up Tennon Street, and when he got to the house he almost collapsed down the steps and into the room in the basement.

Tommy was sitting at the table with a pack of cards, playing Don's records on Don's record player. Tommy looked up.

'Hi, Don!'

Don couldn't answer. Something stuck in his throat that stopped him speaking.

'Something wrong, mate?'

Don turned back up the steps to the passage and went out the front door to the street and motor bike. He got on the bike and revved up the engine. Blindly he started off, gathering speed as he left Tennon Street. Don sped down the long steep hill out of the city. There was not too much traffic about at that moment. A bus was slowly climbing the hill —coming from Derby. There were traffic lights part of the way down the hill, and they were on red. But Don's eyes were blinded with tears and he didn't notice the colour of traffic lights or whether the traffic was light or heavy. There was no traffic crossing the road but it would have been bad luck if there had been. Don raced past the red lights and on down the hill towards Wollaton.

A few minutes later Don was racing against the wind. Now the thoughts in his mind were of his father and a car crashing. And of cars streaming down the M.1. at dusk. A car eating the miles in minutes. Not going anywhere—just going. Lights standing out in the darkness. Each car a lonely-looking world of its own.

Don was speeding along, and the traffic was going too slow for him. Don was speeding past it, into a world of his own, too fast and too far out into the road.

SEVEN

Dion Kilgrady was looking tired and worried. These days he seemed kind of haunted, Jamie thought. Dion had guessed that Jamie must know about Chatterny's identity after the newspaper report.

'So what yer goin' to do, Dee?' Jamie asked, when they had one of their few rare moments alone, one evening.

'Get out as soon as Ernie pays me the money from Wollaton. Things have got worse since that blackmailer tried to squeeze him. He's in a filthy temper most of the time and blames me for everything. He even thinks the blackmailer was me!'

Jamie wanted to laugh out loud, but stopped in time.

'But that's bleddy silly!' he exclaimed. 'You've got enough to worry about wi' out doin' summat like that! Anyway, weren't you with him when the calls came through?'

'No,' said Dion gloomily. 'I was out—not far away, and not for long. But I wasn't there, and that's enough for him.'

That was how Jamie came to persuade Kilgrady to risk his freedom and cheer himself up with a night out with Dolly, Julie and himself. Anyway Julie was asking questions about Kilgrady. Why wasn't he around any more? Where was Dolly? Jamie kept on thinking up excuses, but gave a sigh of relief on the evening Kilgrady actually appeared and went with them to the Classic, New Tennon Street.

It was nearly ten o'clock when they left. Jamie, Julie,

Dolly and Kilgrady followed a young couple out of the cinema and stood on the top step. Apart from two people walking down the road towards Tennon Street there seemed to be nobody else about. It looked like it had been raining but it had stopped now.

'Romantic bull that all was,' Kilgrady commented on the film they had just seen. 'Jaysus, it's nippy.'

'It was a wonderful film,' said Julie, hanging on to Jamie's arm. 'I wish we'd stayed to see the ending again.'

'We were all too hungry to go through it again,' said Kilgrady. 'C'mon. Let's get somethin' to eat.'

Kilgrady turned his coat collar up and they all started to move down the steps. Then Jamie saw it. Something he couldn't stop because he couldn't believe it. A car had slowed down almost to a standstill in the middle of the road, its engine running. From the window of the car a man was taking aim with a gun. Jamie was rigid. Kilgrady saw it instantly and pulled the Darker from his pocket. There was an almighty explosion and Kilgrady fell forwards down the steps. A second explosion came from his own gun as he rolled on to the pavement. With two bullets in him Kilgrady lay dead. The car zoomed down New Tennon Street and was gone.

Jamie bent over Kilgrady and swiftly took the Darker from his hands.

The couple who had come out ahead of them were now about ten yards down the street. They turned to see what all the noise was. The girl screamed. The cinema manager came tearing out of the doors on to the top step, followed by the box-office woman and two usherettes. Someone phoned the police. Lights came on in the windows opposite and people came out of their doors or stood looking from their windows.

Now people were flowing out of the cinema. There were

screams and a lot of noise; a crowd was pressing round Kilgrady and the weeping Dolly who was kneeling over him. People had separated Jamie from Julie. Jamie felt the crowd pushing and shoving behind him. He was on his knees, frozen with shock, watching Dolly screaming, crying and kissing the pale face of Irish Reb. The cinema manager tried to calm her but she was hysterical. Jamie felt Dion's Darker in his pocket. He wanted to be sick. How he wanted to be sick.

He turned round to find Julie. He couldn't see her. He pushed his way up on to the top step and looked down towards Housenal Street. More people were running towards the picture house but there was no sign of Julie in the street.

Then he saw her. Crushed against the side of the steps with her face buried in her hands. He pushed his way through to her.

'Come on, duck, I'm takin' you home,' he said.

'Jamie!' she cried.

'I know,' he said quietly. 'Come on, kid.'

He helped her up and, with his arm round her, they walked slowly away. As they went down New Tennon Street to the Housenal Street bus stop they could hear the noise of police sirens. There was nobody at the bus stop but them.

It was cold. Jamie held Julie close to him and she cried against his shoulder. Her crying gradually grew less and Jamie took out a handkerchief and lifted her head up. He wiped the tears from her cheeks and kissed her. She mumbled, 'Oh Jamie,' and he kissed her again. They seemed to wait for a long time for the bus, and were still the only people at the bus stop when it did arrive. They got on and sat in the first long seats. Jamie paid the bus conductress and told her they were all right when she asked what was up with Julie.

Jamie still felt sick, so did Julie. He started thinking about what had happened. He saw it again in his mind's eye and pictured the face of the assassin. A man of about thirty-nine. Dark hair receding, two chins. There must have been at least two people in the car because he wasn't in the driver's seat. Jamie guessed that it had been the work of Keft. That dirty sonofawhore, nearly out of his mind with fear of Dion leaving him, had convinced himself that Dion was also blackmailing him and had gone to Clint. Clint; whose hatchet man had missed the blackmailer first time, made quite sure he'd get him second time. How did they know where Kilgrady was going to be? Perhaps he had told Keft where he was going? Or maybe they were followed? The car must have been parked half-way down New Tennon Street waiting for Kilgrady to come out so that they could cruise along and pick him off. And maybe miss him and hit Jamie—or Julie or Dolly. Jesus Christ!

He stroked Julie's long hair and kissed her. It was warm and comfortable on the bus and he thought that now there was something for the 'hidden streeters' to talk about. To flash around the town. They'd all know the details in half an hour's time, every one of them. Then the hidden streets wouldn't be hidden any more. Dion's death would be flashed on the front pages of the *Nottingham Evening Post* and would probably find its way into the national papers too, he guessed. How exciting it would all be for the Tennon Streeters. Every telephone in the area would be ringing right now. What a drag for Dion.

Jamie and Julie got off the bus at the city centre and walked to her flat on Lincoln Hill. He held her tight as they came to her door. They'd had time to get cold again and she was trembling as she unlocked the door and went in.

Jamie closed the door, switched on the lamp and the fire. He took her coat off and hung it up, then sat her on the settee. He went into the kitchenette and made her a cup of coffee. He set it down on the table before her.

'It's sweet—how you like it, duck,' he told her. 'I'm just going to the telephone. I'll be back in a minute.'

'Don't be long,' she practically whispered. 'Please.'

Jamie came out of her flat and walked along to the end of the corridor to the covered telephone on the wall. He lifted the receiver and dialled Kilgrady's number.

Somebody at the other end answered. 'Yes?'

'Hello. Keft? 'Oo the 'ell did you think you had killed tonight? Benny? Me? Oh, no! Here I am. Alive and well. Whoever it was who killed Kilgrady was barmy. I'm not the only witness. Three other people saw his face clearly. You shouldn't have had that son of a bitch, Clint, have Kilgrady knocked . . .' Jamie suddenly looked in the telephone booth mirror and saw two men coming up the stairs at the end of the corridor behind him. Both had their hands in their coat pockets. One was *that* man—the assassin. The man who had shot Dion. The other man was Keft. They didn't notice the boy who had his back to them at the telephone. Jamie was alarmed to see them push open the door of Flat J and walk into Julie's room. They closed the door behind them.

'Heyup, 'oo's that?' Jamie cried into the phone. He had completely forgotten his Scottish accent.

There was a laugh at the other end of the line. 'I'm that son of a bitch, Clint.'

Jamie slammed the receiver down. This was frightening. Too bloody dangerous by half. He was travelling too far into nasty, evil ground. He had to pull out.

He lifted the receiver again and dialled the number of the Tennon Street Police Station. 'Hello. I want to speak to somebody high up. It's important. . . Look mate, just hurry up and get someone who'd like ter know where he can get his feelers on Adam Clint. . . Yeh, well come on. Chop, chop. Can't hang about all night. . . Oh, hello. Me? My name's Benny. Now look. Ernest Keft, the "Marry-me" murderer lives at number ten, Flat E, Haven Row Place. If you nip down there pretty swiftly you'll find Adam Clint, if you're lucky. You better move a bit sharpish though. Because summat tells me he ain't gonner be there very long. If you don't find him there you might find him at the Carnden Hotel, wi' some of his middle-aged thugs. Tarar.'

Jamie rang off, ran to Julie's door and put his ear to it.

Keft was saying, 'Now look here, Julie. I don't want to see you hurt. I don't want to see your innocent little lover-boy Jamie hurt, either. But you must forget what you saw tonight. For both your sakes.'

'But why?' screeched Julie, through tears. 'Why did you shoot Dion? What is it all about? Why did Jamie take Dion's gun? Why did Dion have one? Oh, I'm all confused. What am I mixed up in?'

'Jamie took Dion's gun?' asked Keft. His voice seemed urgent there.

'Nothing will happen to you, little girl, if you keep your mouth shut tight,' the other man told her. 'Just forget it, darlin',' and you and Howe will live happily forever after.'

'You're upset,' Keft told her. 'It's been a fierce shock. It hurt me more than it could have hurt Dion. His mother was my sister. You're an innocent girl. You shouldn't get mixed up with Dion's type. You couldn't know what type of a person he was under those silk shirts and fancy suits. Now where's your boy-friend gone? Are you sure Jamie isn't here? We won't hurt him . . . just want to have a talk with him.'

'I've *told* you he's not here,' said Julie. 'He said he was going home.'

'All right, Julie—now forget about what you saw tonight and if you want to keep out of more trouble, stay away from Jamie too.'

'Leave her be,' said the other man. 'Enough has been done for one night. Let's go.'

Jamie dashed back to the telephone and lifted the receiver again. Keft and the man came out of the flat. They closed the door behind them.

'No darlin',' Jamie spoke softly into the receiver, his right hand in his trouser pocket, gripping the Darker tight. 'I can't make it tonight, love.'

The two men's footsteps became fainter as they went down the stairs and out to the street. Jamie dropped the receiver and ran towards Julie's door. He burst into the flat to find Julie lying on her face on the settee, crying.

He walked across to the window and pulled the big yellow curtains to. He walked over to Julie and sat on the floor beside her. He sighed.

'People aren't good, Julie. People are filth. You know what 'appened tonight. Maybe you can't take it in and grasp it yet. But it did 'appen and I think you know why.'

'But I don't, Jamie.'

'Do you know who them blokes was who just left this room?' Jamie asked.

'Dion's uncle,' she said, wiping big tears away with her sleeve. 'The older man was his uncle.'

'Not only was 'e Dion's uncle but 'e was Ernest Keft,' said Jamie. 'Ever heard that name before? Ernest Keft? Well 'e goes about asking young girls to marry him, then he gets money out of 'em and finally he kills 'em. The newspapers call 'im the "Marry-me" murderer and the bloke

115

with him was a professional killer. It was Keft who had Dion killed. And you can't get any lower than our Uncle Ernie Keft. No lower at all.

'I hate people. I despise 'em. All on 'em except you. You're the only person I've been able to get close to. You're the only person I ever wanted to try to understand me. You're the only person I've learned to respect. I don't even respect my parents the way I respect you.'

After that dramatic speech there was silence for a few minutes, then Julie said: 'I saw you take Dion's gun. Why did you do that?'

'Because I want Dion's character clean,' said Jamie. 'I wan' it known that he was unarmed. I wan' it known that he was shot dead in cold blood. Besides,' he added as an afterthought, 'I want to fix Keft.'

'You—you mean—shoot him?' questioned Julie in a jerky voice.

'I'll scare the daylights out on 'im,' Jamie said. 'I can put 'im inside for the rest of his rat-ridden life. If 'e 'ain't already found the coppers at 'ome waiting for 'im.'

'Jamie,' cried Julie, pulling herself round and sitting up. 'Please don't get mixed up in it. If they shot Dion what's to stop them shooting you?'

Jamie stood up straight and pulled out the Darker. 'This. Quite handy for shooting that dirty vermin Keft!'

'Don't be silly,' Julie cried.

'What do you know?' snapped Jamie, and pocketed the gun.

He sat thinking. If I killed Keft and Clint's hired killer, I'd make a big name for myself. I'd be promoted from my image as a thief from Tennon Street to the hero of Tennon Street. But Clint would be after me then. And he'd get me an' all. He'd shoot me in the head and there'd be a crowd of people around me as I lay on my back, quite still. Julie crying and screaming, then fainting. My name and the name of Tennon Street would become famous. I'd be known as a rebel-hero. And what If I'd even managed to shoot Clint dead before one of his pet killers got me? Then I really *would* be a hero. All over England. My face would be flashed up on the news.

Jamie Howe, the teenage rebel who slew gangster chief Adam Clint, one of his bodyguards and the 'Marry-me' murderer, Ernest Keft, was shot dead this evening . . .

Girls would write letters to my mam. I'd be their hero and Julie would get letters of sympathy from females living in different parts of the country. In The Green Leaves car park the Tennon Streeters would scratch on Jamie's wall:

> *Taken away by the devil,*
> *Why did he raise such a fuss?*
> *He proved that he was a rebel.*
> *He roused the rebel in us.*
>
> *The Tennon Street rebel of Notts*
> *Is resting peacefully now.*
> *In a hole, our hero, he rots.*
> *His name was Jamie Howe.*

Railings would be put up around his wall and people would be able to come and read his memorial verse and all the other writing scratched on it.

Suddenly Jamie snapped out of his dream and back to reality. Julie is right in what she is thinking, he said to himself. She knows I couldn't kill anybody.

'Yes,' he said. 'You're right. I might not be able to kill

'im. But I could shake 'im up. Not just for Dion but for you as well.'

'No, Jamie. *Please* keep out of it. I saw Dion killed tonight. It shocked me and I'm dead frightened over it. Especially when two murderers walk straight into my flat and tell me that they'll kill me if I say anything to the police. Jamie, I saw one of our friends shot. What did you see?'

'Red, girl, red is what I saw,' cried Jamie.

Silence for a few long seconds, then,

'Oh *please*, Jamie,' Julie groaned.

Jamie got up to go. He spoke in a quiet voice. 'It's all right, duck. They'll not touch me. Lock your door, take a sleepin' tablet and get some sleep, if you can. I'll see you soon.' He came out of her flat and closed the door behind him. He took his gloves out of his jacket pocket and put them on, turned up his collar and went down the steps and out on to the street. He began to take the slow walk home.

As Wilf Howe was about to go to bed at quarter-past eleven that night, there was a knock on the front door and he opened it. On the door-step stood a man wearing an overcoat and a Robin Hood hat.

'Good evening, sir,' the man said. 'I'm Detective Sergeant Cass of Nottingham C.I.D. Does Jamie Howe live here?'

'Detective?' gasped Wilf. 'Well I'll go to the bottom of our street! I knew it wouldn't last long wi' our kid. Yeh, Jamie Howe is my son. Yer'd best come in.'

Cass stepped in and Wilf closed the door.

'What's it about? What's the lad been up to?' Wilf wanted to know as he took Cass into the living room where Dot was putting curlers in her hair. 'Heyup, Dot, this is a detective come about our Jamie. Mr. Cass, this is my wife Dorothy.'

'Detective?' cried Dot, worried.

'Nothing for you to look so alarmed about, Mrs. Howe,' the man assured her, taking off his hat.

'I knew that lad couldn't go straight,' mumbled Wilf. 'He couldn't stay straight if he was drivin' along the M.I.'

'As far as I know your son hasn't done anything wrong,' said Cass. They all sat down. 'I'm investigating the death of one of his friends. Is Jamie in?'

'No,' said Wilf. 'He went out at about quarter to six to call for his girl-friend. He told us he was taking her to the pictures.'

'Is that Julie Dean?' asked Cass.

'Oh, I dunno 'er name,' said Wilf.

'Yes, Julie, that's what 'e said 'er name was,' said Dot. 'But what's happened ter Jamie's friend? What's Jamie got ter do wi' it?'

'Your son witnessed a murder tonight, Mrs. Howe,' said Cass.

'Oh God!' gasped Dot. 'How terrible! What 'appened?'

'Shots were fired outside the Classic cinema on New Tennon Street at about ten o'clock,' said Cass. 'It resulted in the death of the friend Jamie was with. Jamie and two teenage girls were standing right next to him when he was killed.'

'Who was it?' asked Wilf.

'His name was Dion Kilgrady,' Cass told him.

'That'll be the Mick who brought him home drunk the first night Jamie was home from Kellowyn,' said Wilf.

'Kellowyn?' said Cass.

'Aye, yeh,' said Wilf.

'Borstal, eh?' said Cass. Wilf told him how Jamie had spent two years there but that he had changed since he'd been back and was quite a sensible lad now.

'I don't doubt it, Mr. Howe,' said Cass. 'But you see Kilgrady was under suspicion for robbery, and for being in possession of a gun. He had also been in Kellowyn Court. When we arrived on the scene of the shooting tonight Kilgrady's gun was gone. His girl-friend was there but your son and Julie Dean weren't. Kilgrady's girl-friend gave us a rough outline of what had happened.'

Tennon Street was dark and lonely as Jamie walked down it towards home. I bet everybody knows all about the killing by now, he said to himself. Dion Kilgrady was a rebel. Now he's a dead rebel—a loser. Maybe it was better for him that he didn't exist any more. Things had looked bad for Dion anyway. Everything was loaded against him with Uncle Ernie Keft by his side. But why, Jamie kept asking himself, should Adam Clint have been willing to commit murder on Keft's behalf? What was Keft to Clint? What was the job in London Keft had done for him? Perhaps Keft was more deeply involved in Clint's affairs than he or Dion realized? Perhaps Keft had even been one of Clint's hatchet men in his time? These questions were racing round in Jamie's head, and from somewhere a voice echoed and bounced from wall to wall all the way up Tennon Street: *Not Dion's day. Not Dion's day. Not Dion's day. Not Dion's day.*

At last he came to Deighton Street. The night's too cold to be out in, he thought. He wished he was already in his nice, warm, comfortable bed but he doubted that he'd get any sleep. He was still too shaken and scared to sleep.

He put his hand in his pocket and felt the cold metal of the Darker through his gloves. If only Dion had been a few seconds quicker he might have had a chance, thought Jamie. Now Dion is dead. How does it sound? You was right next to your best mate and he was shot and killed.

The thought made him sick inside again. Made his face stiff with cold and chilled his spine, as he neared the house.

He stopped dead. A grey car was parked outside the gate of his home.

'Coppers!' He stood rigid. Why hadn't he expected it? Of *course* they'd be there, and it would be uncomfortable supplying an excuse for not waiting around for the police after what had happened. And what about the gun? Jamie looked about the dark, deserted street. Where could he hide it? Not in the garden because the scuffs were bound to pull the place apart looking for it.

He started back towards Tennon Street and went down it towards The Green Leaves. The pub looked sad and gloomy in the darkness and there wasn't a sign of life about. He went across the car park. It was empty except for an old Bedford van that had been in the far corner for months. He reached the wall he knew well from when he was a kid— 'Jamie's wall'. He lifted himself up and on to it. Behind he could make out only dark trees and bushes. Beyond were the allotments.

Jamie jumped down into the wet grass. It was too dark to see but he knew exactly where he was. He knew the ground on both sides of 'his' wall. Now he could see the upstairs of the back of the pub. Lights were on but the curtains were pulled. He crept forward, slowly, making his way towards a thick clump of bushes.

His hands were shaking as he started digging a hole in the soil under the bushes with a piece of broken fencing he'd found. He stopped when it was about six inches deep. He took the Darker from his pocket, wrapped it in his handkerchief and laid it in the hole. Then he scraped the soil into the hole again, firmed it down and pulled twigs and leaves over the top. He knew that when he returned for the gun he'd recognize the hiding-place because it was under the first bush past the second tree to the left.

Jamie went back to the wall, climbed it and jumped down into the car park again. His gloves were wet and muddy, his shoes wet and covered with grass. He took the gloves off and used them to wipe the grass and leaves from his trousers and shoes. It was still drizzling with rain and there were a lot of puddles about to account for his soaking wet shoes. He walked up Tennon Street and put the gloves into the first dustbin he came to, burying them under the rubbish.

As he reached Deighton Street he thought about what he might say to the scuffer he knew would be waiting for him. He imagined Wilf would be in a rage, and Jamie would say, 'Heyup, got comp'ny, then?' He'd speak up and his mam would introduce him to Detective Inspector Bobby Copp. Then Detective Inspector Bobby Copp would ask him questions which Jamie would answer with cheek and humour.

The grey car was still there. The sight of it made Jamie more nervous than he intended to be. There was a man sitting in it. A cop. His mate would be inside.

He opened the front gate.

He fiddled about with the door-knocker, taking the key out, unlocking the door and replacing the key inside the lion's head. He went in. The passage light was on. He could hear voices mumbling from the living room. He opened the living-room door and went in. His parents were sitting at the table with the cop.

'Heyup,' he said. 'Got comp'ny?'

'None of yer cheek. There's enough trouble,' said Wilf. The man got up. 'I'm Detective Sergeant Cass.'

'Yeh?'

'You're Jamie, eh?' said Cass.

'Yeh, that's me,' said Jamie.

'You know why I'm here.'

'Yeh, I suppose I do.'

'Shall I get you a cup o' tea, me duck?' Dot asked her son. Then she said to Wilf, 'Ee, look at 'is face. 'E's as white as a sheet.'

'No, no tea thanks, Mam,' said Jamie.

'I'm afraid Jamie will have to come down to the station with me, Mrs. Howe,' said Cass.

'What for, mate?' Jamie asked. 'I've got to be up in the mornin'.'

'A man has been murdered and you'll have to give us a full statement of what you saw, and answer our questions.'

'How long will he be?' asked Dot.

'I don't know. He *may* be able to come back tonight,' said Cass.

Dot and Wilf went to the front door and watched them get into the back of the grey car which quickly drove off towards Tennon Street.

Outside the police station the car stopped and they all got out. Cass led Jamie through a back door. The central heating gave him a sort of comfortable feeling in spite of the edginess that wouldn't leave him. He didn't feel so confident now. He couldn't find his sense of humour and he didn't think his wit and cocky quips would come off.

Cass led him near the door of the C.I.D. room and went across to the desk-sergeant. They were talking for a few minutes, then he came back to him and opened the door of the C.I.D. room. Jamie followed him in and Cass switched the lights on, closed the door and hung his coat up on a hanger.

There were two desks. One had a typewriter on it and

this was the smaller desk. Both had telephones. There was a filing cabinet at the back of the room and three chairs stood at the side.

The bigger desk of the two was in the middle of the room. Besides the telephone there were papers, folders, pens and pencils, different coloured ink in small bottles and a blotting pad. There was also a table lamp. Behind the desk was a chair with a cushion on.

Upon the wall at the end of the room were two large maps. One was of the local area and the other was of the city.

Cass picked up one of the three chairs from the side of the room and dropped it at the bigger desk. He motioned Jamie to sit down on it and then sat down himself on the chair behind the desk.

'Want a cup of tea or summat?' he asked. 'Coffee or chocolate? You ought to. You do look palish.'

'No, ta, I'm all right,' said Jamie.

There was a knock on the door and a plain-clothes man entered. In his hand he held a writing pad and a pencil.

'Jamie, this is Detective Constable Ivan Davis,' said Cass. 'Ivan, this is Jamie Howe.'

Jamie got up then sat down again as Davis pulled up another chair nearer the desk. He prepared himself to write down Jamie's statement.

'Want a cigarette, Jim?' Cass offered.

'No thanks, Mr. Cass,' said Jamie. 'I feel this kind of sickness inside as it is. But if I try to bring it up nowt comes.'

'I was talking to your parents before you came home,' said Cass. 'Talking about you in Kellowyn and what landed you there.'

'Yes?'

'That must have been where you met young Kilgrady,'

said Cass. 'Was it?'

'Yeh, that's right,' said Jamie.

'Well, tell me about you and him and what type of a person you thought he was,' said Cass. 'Tell me how you met up after you came out of Borstal and what you've been doing together since. You know—trips to the pub, flicks, amusement arcades. And anything else you can think of.'

Jamie told him what he knew of Kilgrady's moods and activities in Borstal, and how they had met up in a pub the day after Jamie's release in September. He told him about the dates they'd had with Julie and Dolly, all together. Then Cass asked him to relate what he had seen of the shooting. He had to go through it a couple of times to make sure he hadn't missed out anything the first time. He told Cass everything up to the assassin's getaway.

There was then a few seconds' silence which seemed too long to Jamie.

Then Cass said, 'Did you know that Kilgrady carried a gun around with him?'

Jamie wondered whether it would be safe to say yes. He decided it would be better if he did, so he said:

'Yeh. There's no 'arm in that if 'e's got a licence, is there?'

'He hadn't,' said Cass. 'We've been after him over that gun for a few months. Perhaps it would have worked out better for him if we'd picked him up. We know he carried this Darker gun around all over the place with him. It made him feel big and good. He'd seen too many films.'

'Well, I knew he had it but I never saw it,' said Jamie. 'He told me he had one. I didn't believe him at first, mind, but then I started to.'

'Young Kilgrady liked to be admired,' said Cass. 'He told his friends he had a gun, especially when he'd had too much to drink. He was knocking about with a girl just a few months ago. He took her outside a pub one night and pulled out this gun to show her. Her father was a policeman. He convinced her that he carried it about all the time. Him and his gun never parted. But they did tonight. Tonight his body landed on New Tennon Street. When we went through his pockets there was no gun. It had disappeared. And so had you and your dish. Dolly Benson was hysterical and shrieking your names. She managed to tell us that at first you were there and then you weren't. And she muttered something about you bending down over the body.'

'Like you said,' said Jamie. 'Hysterical.'

'What happened to you and Miss Dean after Kilgrady had fallen?' said Cass.

'I wanted to get Julie home,' said Jamie. 'She was in an 'ysterical state hersen. It was cold and the tears on her cheeks were turning into ice. So I got her home and tried to comfort her.'

'Why didn't you report straight to the police?' snapped Cass.

'I thought it could wait till the mornin',' said Jamie. 'I told Dolly to tell the police that I'd pop round in the mornin'. Then I took Julie 'ome. I could hardly stop mesen from pukin' me inside up.'

Cass sighed. 'Would you recognize the killer if you saw him again?'

'Prob'bly,' said Jamie.

'What did he look like? Describe him to me.'

'He was in a car and that dun't help,' Jamie told him. 'He was just ordinary. Double-chinned, but ordinary features. But I'm sure I'd recognize 'im if I saw him kickin' about this way again.'

'We're having some photographs sent up for you to look

at,' said Cass. 'We'll see if we can find our killer among them.'

'Oh,' said Jamie. 'All right.'

Cass sat there and fiddled about with his ball-point pen in silence for a few minutes. The silence seemed so long and drawn out it began to worry Jamie. Then,

'What have you done with Kilgrady's gun, Jim?' The question came so quietly and suddenly it frightened Jamie. He wasn't expecting it—it had caught him off his guard. He felt his face burning red and told himself: Be careful, you bloody fool. Prepare yourself for moves like that and don't get into an urgent, panicky state. Old Bobby Copp is only guessing and he can't prove a thing.

'What have I done wi' *what?*' he cried. ''Is *gun?* W-w-wha' der yer mean?'

Cass leaned forward with his elbows resting on the desk.

'Where did you hide it? In the front garden? You took it didn't you?'

'No!' cried Jamie, managing an offended expression on his face.

'We can search, yer know,' said Cass. 'The garden, the house.'

'So search away, Mr. Cass,' said Jamie. 'You'll find nowt.'

'Get up,' Cass said.

'What, sir?'

'Get up!' snapped the copper, getting nasty all of a sudden. Jamie did as he was told. 'Empty your pockets out.' Jamie took out his money, a handkerchief, a bus ticket, half a cinema ticket, a box of matches and a packet of cigarettes and put them on the desk.

'Frisk him,' Cass commanded Davis. The other man got up and put his pencil and pad on the desk. Cass said to Jamie. 'Raise your arms.' He then got up and walked round the desk to Jamie's side.

Jamie raised his arms and Davis ran his hands up Jamie. He finished and shook his head at Cass. Jamie lowered his arms.

'I don't want any of your bloody nonsense,' Cass said roughly. 'Where is it? What did you do with it? Why did you take it, lad? Plan to pull a few jobs on your lonesome?'

'I don't know what the 'ell you're talkin' about, sir, I swear it,' Jamie insisted.

'I bet you don't,' grunted Cass, shoving him back in the chair. Cass turned away to face the wall-map. 'Where does Julie Dean live?'

'Lincoln Hill. Number 14 J.'

'Did you leave the gun there?' snapped Cass, digging his hands into his trouser pockets.

'Honest, I never even seen it,' Jamie persisted.

'We can search her flat,' Cass said, turning back to face him.

'You won't be able to get in tonight,' said Jamie. 'She was upset and was goin' to take sleepin' pills to mek 'er sleep. Anyroad, you can search the whole place but you'll not find a gun.'

'No?' said Cass, sitting on the edge of the desk. 'But we'll find it soon. If you took it we'll find it. You can make it easier by telling us now. Easier for you, easier for us. But if we find you've hidden it after you not telling us then you are in *real* trouble.'

A uniformed policeman came in then. He handed Cass a folder then went out. Cass took a pile of cards out of the folder. They had photographs on them. He set them down, on the desk, in front of Jamie.

'Look at them carefully and see if you can find the face of the man who killed Kilgrady tonight.'

'Coppers!' Jamie said to himself as he took a look at the face and profile of the first man. Thee mek you sick!

The next day was Friday. Julie didn't wake up until gone ten o'clock. She climbed out of bed and slipped a dressing gown over her soft body. She opened the flat door and picked up a package that had been left outside by the postman, then came inside again and closed the door. She carried the package into the kitchenette and unwrapped it to find four advance copies of *Woman's Play*. In this issue was her very first success: 'J'y suis, j'y reste'.

While she made herself a cup of tea, she looked up her own story in the top copy. There it was, with a drawing to illustrate her hero and heroine by Blanche Dreer. The picture was quite a disappointment but it was nice to see her name in print.

As she drank her tea, her head began to clear, and the memory of the night before came back like a bad dream. This was the moment she'd been living for: to see her first story in published form. But now it had come, she couldn't feel happy or enjoy her success. No, not now. Julie was stunned and frightened. Suppose those two men came back? Suppose the police wanted to question her?

The doorbell rang. She started and sat still and rigid. The bell rang again, and she heard Dolly's voice.

'Julie, it's me! C'mon Julie—open up!'

Julie hurried to let her in. Dolly looked pale and haggard.

'Yeh, I know I look rough, but I 'aven't bin ter sleep,' she said as she came in.

'Come and have some tea, love,' said Julie. 'Sit down.'

Dolly sat down heavily on the settee and Julie brought the tea and sat beside her.

'Where d'you an' Jamie go after . . . when the police

came?' Dolly said.

'Jamie brought me home here. It was all so awful, and I was by myself . . . in that crowd. Then Jamie got me away from it and we got on a bus and came back. I had two sleeping pills. But what about you? What happened?'

'I don't really know,' said Dolly. 'I only remember Dion fallin' down, an' all those people, an' the police station an' questions. Oh, my God!' And she began to cry again.

Presently Dolly calmed down, wiped her eyes and went on:

'But I've got to face up to it. Poor Dion. He really—*really* is dead. And things've bin made badder. He's taken 'issen to the grave wi' a bad name. He tried to think he was first-class but he wasn't. He was second-rate.'

'Second-rate what, love?' Julie asked her.

''Im—an' Jamie—an' Charlie,' said Dolly. 'All three on 'em. Second-rate crooks.'

'What are you talking about?' said Julie.

'Oh you *must* know,' said Dolly, scratching the back of her neck. 'Their little racket.' Julie's head was reeling.

'*What* little racket, Dolly? What do you mean?'

'Well you must know about Jamie's two years in Borstal. Yeh, an' he'll be back there again before the year's out, an' all.'

Julie tried to take a grip on herself. Try not to be too surprised, she kept thinking. Try. It's a disappointment, yes, but *try*.

'Didn't yer know?' said Dolly. 'Ah. Dion's bin inside an' all. That's where the two on 'em met.'

Julie groaned, 'I didn't even know Dion was crooked. I don't know who Charlie is, either.'

'Oh, Charlie's the thug who's Dion's uncle,' Dolly said in a tired voice. 'At the police station last night they checked up on Jamie. As if they really needed to! The desk-sergeant knew his name straight off. All the trouble he'd had with him when he was a kid! Dion told me that Jamie was supposed to have assaulted a girl in her own home and swiped forty-eight nicker from her house when he was about sixteen.'

'No, it's not true!' exclaimed Julie. 'It can't be!'

'Tennon Street brings 'em up like that, duck,' said Dolly. 'None of 'em gives a tinker's cuss about anything. They say that Jamie always thought he was God Almighty 'Issen. Always had to be at the centre of attention.'

Julie felt there was something unreal about the way they talked. As if they were speaking over a long-distance telephone and couldn't see each other.

The doorbell rang again. Julie went to the door to find a weary-looking man there, presenting his credentials as Detective Sergeant Dudley Cass. She let him in and closed the door.

'My colleague called very early this morning,' he informed her, 'and I called later.'

'I'm sorry. But I took sleeping pills last night and I didn't wake up till ten.'

'Good morning, Miss Benson,' he smiled as he saw Dolly. 'I hope you're feeling better.'

'Thanks,' she said. 'A bit tired. But you don't look none too bright, yoursen.'

'I've been on duty most of the night,' said Cass.

'I suppose now we shall 'ave to go ter Dion's send-off party,' said Dolly bitterly. 'Dion always said his send-off 'ud be a bloody good un.'

'Would you like a cup of tea, Mr. Cass?' asked Julie.

'Er, yes please,' he said.

'Yeh,' groaned Dolly. 'Well, I must go, Julie. Thanks for the tea.'

Dolly got up and Cass listened for the flat door to close before he spoke. Julie poured him some tea.

'Are you feeling all right this morning, Miss Dean?'

'I feel exhausted,' she admitted. 'I feel shattered, like I won't be able to go on through the day, and I feel worse and worse each minute.'

'I'm sorry,' said Cass. He paused, drank his tea, then said: 'I'm afraid I shall have to ask you some questions about yourself and about last night.'

'Yes.'

'Do you live here alone?'

'Yes.'

'Do you work?'

'I work in a wool shop four mornings a week,' said Julie. 'My father pays the rent of this flat and makes me an allowance of money. I want to succeed as a writer and he's trying to help me. He's convinced that one day I shall write a bestseller so I won't need any more financial help. So far I've only had one short story published by a magazine.' She dropped her hand down on the magazines.

'How very interesting,' said Cass. He paused for a while and Julie said nothing more to fill the gap of silence. At last he said, 'You are a friend of Jamie Howe?'

'Yes,' she said, sitting back. 'You know I was standing right next to him last night outside the Classic. Why else would you be here?'

'What made you run?' asked Cass.

'Run?' she said. 'I didn't run anywhere. I was upset, terribly upset. Jamie walked me down the street. I was too helpless and confused to stop him. I couldn't take it in properly.'

'Did Jamie run his hands through Dion's pockets?' Cass asked. 'Did he bend down and take anything from him?'

She wasn't sure how to handle this without giving Jamie away.

'I—I don't know,' she said. 'I can't remember. I was so shocked and confused I couldn't take in what was happening.'

'How long have you known Jamie Howe?' Cass questioned.

'Since—since September,' said Julie.

'Did you see the man in the car?'

'Pardon?'

'The man who fired.'

'I told you,' she cried, 'I couldn't take in *anything*.'

Cass rubbed his tired eyes. 'You'd better pack some things and go and stay with your parents for a while, Miss. But first, I'd like you to come down to the station to make a statement.'

'Why should I go to my parents for a while?' Julie asked.

'Just to be on the safe side,' said Cass. 'I'll take you there, after you've been to the station.'

'All right,' she said, standing up. 'Let me get dressed first.'

'Of course,' he said. 'There's no hurry. I'll wait for you.'

She went into the bedroom and closed the door. He heard her dragging a suitcase across the floor. In half an hour he escorted her to the police car waiting outside.

The police had let Jamie go home that night and he had gone to work next day. At knocking-off time Jamie walked up Tennon Street from Hadley Yard towards New Tennon Street. On the way up he called into Vincent Bilco News-agents and bought an *Evening Post*. Dion Kilgrady's face stared up at him beneath the headline: *Shot dead outside cinema*. Then followed an account of what happened. The other big topic on the same page was the report of the arrest of Adam Clint, which Jamie enjoyed reading as he sat on the bus he caught from Housenal Street.

From the city centre Jamie walked to Lincoln Hill and to Julie's flat door. He rang the bell and spent the next five minutes playing 'Jingle Bells' on it but she wasn't there. So he came home.

At about twenty to nine that night Jamie was watching television. He decided he wanted company. He wanted Julie's company but he didn't feel like going over there again. Dion was dead. Those three words still spun round dizzily in his head when he said them. They'd been spinning round all day. There was nobody to go drinking with now, and he needed somebody to back him up. A group of friendly people that liked and respected him. This mood had been absent for two years, but now it was back. He wanted to lead his old gang again. But his gang weren't kids any more and they wouldn't be sitting on 'his' wall again.

So he left the telly, put his cap and jacket on and walked up Deighton Street. It was raining, not heavily, just a drizzle. He arrived at The Green Leaves and was glad to step into its warm atmosphere out of the cold. Some of the old gang were standing about the counter. Trev was the first to notice him. 'Heyup, kidder,' he shouted. 'Come to join the party?'

'Just thought I'd pop in,' Jamie said, unzipping the front of his jacket. 'Nowt on telly. So for the sake o' summat ter do . . .'

'What's this I've 'eard about your Irish mate bein' shot off top steps at flicks?' asked Trev.

Jamie wanted to tell them about everything. About Keft and Clint. He wanted their admiration. But all he could tell them was the Dion Kilgrady story from the time they met in Kellowyn to the night before, leaving out the bits about Keft and Clint.

'I bet last night was just about all you could take, wa'n't it?' said Doreen.

'No,' Jamie assured her. 'I took my girl-friend home, comforted her and came home to find a detective waiting for me. He asked questions and I answered with comedy.'

'Yeh-heh,' roared Trev with a grin. 'Yo' war allus good for cheekin' rosses off wi' funny talk.'

'Tennon Street's got a bad name as it is,' said Lynn, 'without a bloke gerrin' murdered up this way.'

''Ere, Missis,' Trev yelled up to the barmaid. 'Come on! Get down 'ere an' do some work for a change.'

When Jamie had got his ale they all went to the tables with their drinks. All laughed gaily at each other's jokes but Jamie didn't. Things seemed different. He couldn't join in. He sat supping his ale without making a sound, just politely smiling. Trev was the centre of attention now. It was him who cracked the best jokes, him who laughed the loudest and him who impressed the girls. Jamie had seen himself in Trev's place. One time he had been. Jamie had reigned high on his wall outside. But now he just sat silent with one hand gripping a glass and the other arm over the back of the chair.

None of the gang seemed to notice how quiet Jamie was. They didn't even look at him as they took their drinks off the trays of drinks he paid for. When his turn came round again he got up and went to the counter to order more. As he stood in the crowd waiting he felt a tugging at his elbow. He looked down behind him and saw a small, stocky man dressed in rough clothes. He was rather like a tramp. He had a brown moustache and beard that seemed slightly out of place on such a scruffy character because the beard looked well-cared for. Then the man whispered, 'Jamie, Jamie.'

'Do you know me?' said Jamie.

'Come on,' said the tramp. 'With me. In the gents.'

'Eh?'

The tramp turned away and Jamie followed him into the toilets. The toilets were empty and the tramp made sure of this by opening the door of each compartment.

'What's the idea?' said Jamie. ''Oo the 'ell are you?'

'Me, Charles,' said the tramp, turning from the last toilet door to face him.

'Christ,' cried Jamie. 'That's a lovely disguise.'

'You know Dion's dead,' said Keft.

'Yeh,' said Jamie. 'I was there when it 'appened.'

Keft went on: 'Two of Adam Clint's boys got picked up at our flat the same night Dion died. After the cops had been round the flat and picked them up they went off down to the Carnden and arrested Adam Clint and his son and one or two other blokes I think. I wasn't there or they'd have pulled me in and that could be unhealthy, too.'

Aye, I bet it could an' all, thought Jamie.

'Clint's friends will be out for me if he gets sent down,' said Keft, worried. 'They'll think I tipped off the police. And if they don't have enough to pin Clint down with then Clint himself will be out after me. He can get me killed. He would, I know he would.'

'Did you?'

'Tip the law off? Jesus, no.'

Jamie looked concerned. 'You was mad ter stick about Nottingham, anyroad. I can't see what there was here for you—bloke with your brains for jobs. Look what Nottingham did for Dion. I'd clear off out of it if I was you. But

136

first I want my cut. We split the loot in two and then we part and go our different ways. Agreed?'

'Splendid by me,' said Keft. 'In fact I've got a man who is going to buy half of our stock. We're to meet him on Sunday. That's why I've been looking for you. To tell you.'

'How did you know where I'd be?' said Jamie.

'Never mind that now—I've got to go,' said Keft. 'Come to Vic Sandford's scrap-yard by the canal on Bonnow Street, Sunday at nine o'clock. We'll be meeting Mr. Wesson there. And by sometime next week I'll have me goods packed and I'll be gone.'

'Are you living in Wollaton now that the cops have taken your flat?' Jamie asked. Keft said he was and Jamie asked for the address. With the address all written down, safely in his pocket, Jamie returned to the others with the drinks.

Nobody said he'd been a long time, in fact nobody was saying anything. They'd all gone quiet. 'Heyup, what's the marrer?' he said as he handed the drinks round. Then he saw that someone else had joined them: a fair-haired, thick-set boy he'd never seen before. Trev looked up.

'Ah, thanks, Jamie. Jamie, this is Tommy Bryan. Tommy's just told us some bad news about Don.'

'Oh, that gink,' mumbled Jamie. 'What is it?'

'He was killed on his motor bike out at Bramcote,' Trev said.

Jamie stood in shocked silence. Then, after a time he whispered, 'What—what happened? To Don.'

Tommy took a deep breath. 'From what I've heard he was speeding up the A.52, tearing round the roundabout to go down Nottingham Road through Bramcote and to Stapleford when he hit a lorry coming off the dual carriageway. He died just before the ambulance arrived.'

Jamie swallowed.

'When did it 'appen?'

'Wednesday evening.'

Jamie couldn't speak.

He turned his back on them, walked towards the door, and out into the cold, soothing drizzle of the night.

EIGHT

Bonnow Street is a very short street running down to the canal path. It starts at the corner shop and ends at number nine. Opposite number nine, on the left-hand side, is the property owned by *Vic Sandford and Sons, Scrap Merchants*. The canal path runs past the scrap-yard and past the bottom of the street.

On the Sunday night following Kilgrady's death, Bonnow Street was dark and cold. The only light was supplied by a street lamp which shone over a sign warning people that the canal was at the bottom of the street.

Jamie, with a scarf round his neck and gloved hands in his coat pockets, his right hand around the butt of the gun, came ambling along and turned the corner into Bonnow Street. At the same time a lad he knew came out of number three. It was Bob Denham. He closed the front door, stuck his hands in his coat pockets and started walking towards Jamie, looking downwards. Because he was looking downwards he didn't see Jamie until they knocked into each other. They both looked up.

'Sorr—*Jamie*!' cried Bob. 'Jamie Howe!'

'Heyup!' grinned Jamie, sounding as surprised as Bob was. 'How you limpin' along?'

'Ah, pretty well,' laughed Bob. ''Ere, where've *you* bin playin' wi' yoursen? You've been out o' Kello for years now an' Ah've not seen you about. But I 'eard about your latest adventure—on Thursday, outside flicks. Rough.'

'Yeh,' said Jamie. ''E wa' a mate o' mine. We'll talk about it some time, Bobby, kid. I've got ter goo now.'

'Where y' off round 'ere?' Bob wanted to know.

'I'm goin' ter see someone,' said Jamie.

'Yeh?' said Bob. 'I've just come out our cousin's place. Number three. We've been puttin' his ale away inside us in their front room all afternoon an' after tea.'

'Lucky devil,' said Jamie.

'Ah, norrarf,' Bob laughed. 'Anyroad, I'll see yer sometime, Jamie. Tarar.'

'See yer.'

Bob walked on and disappeared around the corner.

Jamie came to the open gates of the scrap-yard. He went through into the darkness. He'd been by here in the daytime once. When he was a kid. It had seemed to be a smallish yard. He was just about able to make out the figure of a man standing by Vic Sandford's truck which was parked near the railings that divided the canal path from the scrap-yard. He couldn't see him clearly but he knew it was Keft. He walked over to him.

'Heyup, Charlie,' Jamie said, 'where's yer mate Wesson?'

'Ah, he's gone. But it's all fixed.'

'I thought you was goin' ter wait for me before you settled it? I'm not late.'

'He couldn't stay.'

'Well, is 'e goin' to tek the loot?'

'Half of it.'

'How much?' asked Jamie.

'Six hundred.'

Jamie looked gone-out. 'I thought you told me that me an' you would get about a thousand each for what we had in that house. If Wesson takes half of it, we should get five hundred each.'

'Six hundred is all Wesson's—clients—are willing to give for it,' said Keft. 'Anyway he's given me a hundred now and the rest when he collects the goods.'

'Six hundred!' Jamie moaned. 'I bet 'e thinks 'e's very clever. Fancy pullin' a fast one like that. An' you lettin' 'im.'

'I don't care,' said Keft. 'All I want is a bit of money and to be gone. That's half of the stuff got rid of.'

'Well what about my half of the hundred?'

'Yes,' said Keft, 'let's go over there where there's some light and I'll give it you.'

Jamie turned away to lead on. After a few paces forward he stopped dead. He felt something small and hard digging into the middle of his back. He turned to see what it was but Keft's voice from behind ordered, 'Don't turn round. Just keep strollin' until you get to the door of the office.'

'A gun!' cried Jamie, cold with shock. He had intended being the one to pull a gun first. He shook with fright. His inside was paralysed with fear of what this criminally insane man might do to him. Am I going to die? Jamie asked himself. Three days after Dion, four days after Don. Would the sun rise and the bright blue sky shine down to find his corpse in the scrap-yard as the city came back to life? Would everybody wake up except for him? He felt dizzy. The darkness began to spin around him. He tried to bring himself to ask Keft if he had come to the scrap-yard just to kill him, but the only sound he was able to manage was a croak.

'Move, son,' commanded Keft, pushing him forward with the gun. Jamie stepped forward into a whirlpool of air. A million thoughts travelled through his mind. A parade of faces, names and places going at a speed too fast for him to catch and recognize. He stepped forward clumsily; he wept silently, wondering where and when it would happen, and hoping that he would never know, that the bullet would take him by surprise and that pain would not linger. He hoped he wouldn't have to think about it and realize that dying was a nasty hell of a feeling.

Then he stumbled and rolled on to the ground. It was a lucky accident. An explosion shook the cold night air and a flame flashed from Keft's gun. Jamie's mind was numb, but his body seemed to work on its own. The Darker warmed the palms and fingers of his right hand while he lay leaning on his left elbow pointing the gun upwards. The gun went off. It seemed to jump slightly as the explosion deafened him. He had fired too soon without taking aim but he had scared Keft out of sight.

Tears trickled down Jamie's cheeks. He bawled out, stammering, 'Ah'm—Ah'm—Ah'm gonner kill you, Keft! I'm Benny the blackmailer and I'm gonner kill you for what you did to Dion, and to my Julie. You're dead, you whore's son, you son of a stupid bitch.'

Then he scrambled for cover behind a mountain of junk. Behind a big old bath he crouched, all tense, waiting. He felt a slight relief now that he had a chance, though he gripped the gun so tight that it hurt the palm of his hand. He was sweating and the gun was sticky and warm.

For a long time he waited for a sound. None came. Then, after a while, he was sure a sound came from behind him. It jolted his inside for him. Jamie froze with horror, waiting for everything to end. His heart beat faster and louder. No other sound followed and he began to wonder how alive his imagination was as his heart slowed down to a steady pace.

He peered out into darkness to try and catch a movement

or something that would give him an idea of where Keft was. But there was nothing. The only sound was that of distant traffic going over the canal bridge. Jamie wished that he was at home in bed falling asleep or kissing Julie and stroking her long hair as she leaned next to him.

No, he mustn't let his mind wander like this. Suddenly— crash!

To his left came the noise of clattering metal. It made him jump like hell. He spun halfway round and fired blindly. Then he saw Keft picking himself up from the scrap he had kicked over. Jamie could just make out the features of his face. Keft held up his gun and fired, hitting the old bath behind Jamie. This jolted Jamie's inside, too, and his finger smothered the trigger of the Darker. *Crack!*

Keft swayed. Jamie gasped. Keft fell backwards, slowly, with his arms loose like a rag doll. Jamie had never been so frightened in all his life. The atmosphere—the world— everything was unreal.

Keft had fallen behind the scrap metal he had first kicked over as he had been creeping round from a truck. Since his fall only seconds had passed, but it seemed like hours without a sound or movement from either of them.

Jamie got to his feet. Inside he felt sick and empty. He walked slowly to where Keft had fallen. He stopped; he looked down. Ghastly sight! It made him giddy, weak. He heaved, he dropped the gun and fell to his knees. He cried.

Keft was lying on his back. He couldn't be anything but dead. One bullet! Just one bullet had ripped his face apart! His face was a mass of blood, split with cracked skin. Half of his nose, his right eye and some of his right cheek was gone. The left eye stared upwards. It was terrifying—worse than anything out of a horror film.

Now there were voices. Shouts from people in the street

who had heard the firing. Soon the police would arrive. He must get away quick. Not the way he'd come. The other way, over the railings to the canal bank. He blundered across the yard, following a sort of path between the mountains of scrap. Somehow he reached the railings and got over them. He dropped down into the dark of the canal bank, crying. He fell to his knees and vomited into the water. For quite a while he was sick, and when he thought he had finished he stumbled on towards the nearest bridge but he didn't get far before he spewed into the water again. He was sick a couple more times before reaching the nearest way out to the streets.

When he found the streets he walked where it was dark. He walked and walked, not knowing where he was going. At last, he didn't know how long—he'd lost all sense of time—he found himself on Winchester Street. Lincoln Hill was two streets away. He had been walking unsteadily and weakly but now he was a little stronger. The thought of Julie soothed his empty mind. He came to the top of Lincoln Hill and looked down the other side. Slowly he carried on his way down until he came to the flats at number 14.

Jamie climbed the stairs, with some effort, and reached the second floor. He leaned against the door of Flat J and pressed the white button that rang the bell. When nobody answered he groaned and rang again. Still nobody came.

'Help me, Julie,' he moaned, '*help me*!' Jamie hammered on the door with his fists. 'Please, let me in! Help me!'

The door of Flat H opened and a small middle-aged man in shirt-sleeves and braces came out. 'Heyup, what's gooin' on 'ere?' he demanded.

Jamie looked over his shoulder and murmured that the man was to shut his gob before he made elastic bands out of his lips.

The man could see how rough he looked. 'Less o' that kind of talk or there'll be trouble. What's up wi' yer?'

'Nowt.'

'Der yer want a doctor or summat?'

'Leave me alone.'

'What's wrong wi' yer then?'

The man was irritating Jamie. Jamie brought his fist crashing down on Julie's door. 'Leave me *be*! Mind yer own business.'

'All right, all right,' the man cried. 'Go away then an' stop mekin' all this noise or Ah'll call the police ter yer.' He went back in his own flat and closed the door.

Jamie pressed his face against Julie's door. But a voice inside him told him she wasn't there. She was at her mother's.

He pushed himself away from the door and moved down the passage to the telephone on the wall. He stuck his right hand in his trouser pocket, pulled out his small diary and shakily flicked through the pages until he found Julie's parents' phone number. He then took some coins out of his trouser pocket and phoned their number.

Mrs. Dean answered. Jamie told her who he was and asked if he could speak to Julie. A minute later he heard Julie's voice. 'Jamie?'

'Julie!' he almost sobbed. 'Julie, I need you to—to—oh, my Christ, help me!'

'Jamie, what is it?' she cried.

'Julie—' he groaned. It was hard trying to tell her. It was tormenting. 'I—I killed a man—tonight, I *killed* a man.'

'What are you saying?'

'He's dead—destroyed . . .'

'Jamie, where are you?'

'Out—Ah'm—Ah'm outside your flat,' he told her. 'Come

an' 'elp me—'

'Wait there, Jamie. I'll be there as soon as I can,' she told him. 'I'll borrow my dad's car and you keep quiet and calm until I get there.'

She rang off and the telephone purred into his ear. 'Julie,' he murmured, wishing that her voice would return to talk to him. When it didn't he replaced the receiver and went back to her door and leaned on it.

The next twenty minutes seemed like a life-time. Nobody came out of any of the other flats and the only sound was a television coming from somewhere.

Jamie's mind pictured the dead Keft and he felt sick again.

Then footsteps came running up the stairs: tap-tap-tap, and Julie appeared on the landing. The buttons of her grey-blue coat were undone.

'Jamie!' She came towards him. He looked terrible. His hair was tangled and damp with sweat. His face was white except for the red about his eyes. He didn't go to hold her, he just pointed to the door.

She took out her key and unlocked the door, telling him how she had dashed to get here, nearly jumping the lights at Slab Square. She opened the door. Jamie pushed his way in front of her and threw himself into the bathroom.

When Jamie came out of the bathroom, feeling like all the strength in his legs had gone, he saw her hanging her coat up on the hanger on the door. She was dressed in a short dark blue skirt and a light blue roll-neck sweater, and she turned and came across to him and rested her hands on his shoulder. Her big blue eyes looked up at him with a kind of sad expression about them which was familiar to him.

'Tell me . . . about it,' she said, almost in a whisper.

146

She put her arms around his neck and he put his around her waist and held her near to him. She felt him trembling against her.

Jamie began to feel warm again. Her being so close to him and their holding on to each other gave him a feeling of security. After what had happened he knew that Julie was the only person he could talk to about it. And the nice, clean, fresh smell of her made him feel good.

She broke away from him and took him into the kitchenette. There he sat at the table while she made some tea. He told her what he'd done and how it happened. He stopped in the middle of it all to complain of a headache, so Julie opened the cupboard and took out some aspirins. She gave him a glass of water to swallow two down with.

When Julie had finished making the tea she sat down at the other side of the table and watched him go whiter in the face as he described the terrible sight of the dead Ernest Keft.

'Drink your tea, love,' she said, in a whisper.

He sipped the tea. It was strong.

'It's funny,' he said. 'You spend half your life acting so big. Showing off to impress the world—to capture people's admiration for you. Half your life being somebody you ain't. . . . And you don't realize how lonely you really are. Nobody really cares. They 'aven't been taking any notice of you for all the years yer've bin showin' off. You find that the only person you've been kidding is yourself.

'I used ter think killin' a man would be easy whenever I saw it 'appen at the pictures, when I was a kid. In a way I suppose it is. You don't pull the trigger—your nerves do, your brain does. You're hardly conscious of it. You're wondering whether you should kill him or not at the same second you're doing it.

'I wandered through the streets gettin' 'ere. I dunno what wa' runnin' through me mind at that time. It seemed all jumbled up wi' things. Pictures and words all crashed up against each other. It must be that what's gen me a 'ead-ache.'

Julie moved her hand across the table and held his right hand. 'Jamie! Why? Why did you get mixed up with these people?'

He covered her hand with his left hand. He forced tears back behind his eyes as he said, slowly and quietly, 'I'm sorry, kid. I'm sorry.'

'Jamie,' she said. 'Did—did anybody see you?'

'Nah,' he told her. 'I shouldn't think so. Ha, when you think of how I got into it! I wandered so far into the under-world that I found I had to kill to get out of it. I'm a common thief turned murderer.'

'Stay clean now, Jamie,' Julie said, sort of pleading.

'There's some things at Wollaton I've got to get rid of,' he said, looking down. 'But after that I will, I swear it.' He looked up and moaned, 'Oh, I've still got this 'eadache, Julie.'

'Give it time.'

'I can't go 'ome,' he told her.

'Why?'

'I can't,' he said. His eyes were stinging as tears tried to escape again.

Julie's hand came over his again. 'You can stay here for as long as you feel you have to. For as long as you like.'

'Thanks, Julie,' he said. 'Oh, my 'ead 'urts. I'll not be able to sleep.'

'I'll—I'll let you have a sleeping pill,' she said. 'I'll go back to my parents for the night and you can sleep in my bed-room here.'

'Don't go.'

'My father's car is outside,' said Julie. 'I must take it back, he'll need it in the morning. But I'll come back tomorrow before nine o'clock.'

'Julie, you're wonderful,' he smiled faintly, and rubbed the tears from his cheeks.

Jamie had taken a sleeping pill and now he lay in Julie's bed with the sheets up to his chin. There was no light on in the room. The door was open, though, and the light was on in the living room. He could just make out a black figure that was Julie standing by the bed. She leaned over him and kissed his forehead. She said good-night and then she went out of the room and closed the door. A few minutes later all the lights went out. He heard her close the flat door. And he slept.

At half-past eight next morning Julie let herself into her flat, carrying her typewriter. She closed the door behind her, then stood the typewriter on the coffee table and hung her coat up on the hanger on the door. She went into the bedroom. Jamie was asleep.

He didn't wake up until ten. By then Julie had been to the shops in the city centre to get some food. She had decided not to go to work today.

She made him breakfast and he sat at the table in his bare feet. Then he gave her the phone number of the firm his father worked for and she went out to the telephone. She phoned Wilf and told him that Jamie had a stomach upset and would be spending a few nights at her parents' house.

Jamie felt ill for most part of the day. He sat in the armchair, watching Julie typing. He didn't speak much and sometimes his mind wandered away into deep thought. Several times he started sweating as pictures of the night before ran through his mind. The fear—the nerves—the noise.

The only real thing he was aware of was the faint, distant tapping that was Julie's typewriter.

At tea time Julie went out to buy a newspaper. He saw her going out but he hadn't heard her telling him where she was going and didn't bother to ask. She wasn't gone long. When she came back they read what the paper had to say about 'the murdered man found in a scrap-yard' together. Julie sat on the arm of his chair. He held the newspaper and she read the passage out loud. The report told them that the dead man had not yet been identified but that the murder gun had been found near the body. Julie took the paper away from him.

'God, Jamie,' she gasped. 'You shouldn't have left it.'

He groaned. 'Christ. Finger prints.'

'What are we going to do?'

'We? I killed 'im, you didn't. Oh Christ.'

'It was self-defence Jamie. You would never have killed him if he hadn't tried to kill you.'

'Be 'ard ter prove. Ah'll goo down fer murder if Ah'm caught.'

There was silence for a while.

'What . . . what would you like for tea?' Julie asked.

'Nowt. I don't wan' owt!'

'Jamie.'

But he didn't take anything. He even let the cup of tea she made him get cold. She had to throw it all away.

At about eight o'clock Julie sat on the settee, resting her chin on her hands, drifting into the same sort of mood that he was in. He looked up and said, 'If I'm making you miserable I'll go home.'

'No.'

A few minutes later: 'I'll go.'

'You can stay. I said you could.'

He got up and went to the hanger. He put his coat on and said, 'Thanks, kidder. P'raps I'll see yer sometime next week. Tarar.'

The door closed. He had gone. She sat in a kind of trance, unable to move in the atmosphere he'd left behind. After a while she switched on the television to try to bring her back to reality. But it was unbearable and she switched it off again. Had she failed Jamie when he needed her? Where had she gone wrong? She had tried so hard to understand the facts about Jamie—everything she'd learned in the last few days—but it was all so bewildering. Jamie must have sensed that she didn't *really* understand at all. He must have been disappointed in her. But what would happen to him? Where had he gone? He would be feeling lost and lonely and she wouldn't be there to help him.

Julie realized that things would never be the same. And she was right. They never saw each other again.

NINE

On Tuesday morning, the following day, the police picked Jamie up at the Wollaton house with what was left of the stolen goods. Somebody had broken into the house before Jamie and he guessed that it might have been Wesson's people—if Wesson ever existed. They had taken all the stuff they could find and carry except for two suitcases which Jamie imagined they intended returning for. The police discovered Jamie unwrapping jewellery from bits of cloth out of the suitcases.

At the police station he decided the only thing he could do was to admit that he had stolen the jewellery. Outside the sun was shining and he felt extra hot and sweaty. No matter how hard he tried he wasn't able to think of something good to explain his being found with stolen property, to get him out of it. His mind was jumping from one picture to another. Kilgrady dying, Keft dying, darkness, fear, tense atmosphere, Kilgrady's confident grinning face, Kilgrady dead, Dolly screaming, Julie crying, Keft dead. He didn't hear all that the police said to him. The only thing that he could tell them was that he stole the goods from places in and around Nottingham. And he did it alone. He told them he was a strict loner.

In the afternoon, at about two o'clock, he was driven to Tennon Street's police station where he was taken into a room to meet Chief Inspector Hophey. Jamie was left alone in a room, sitting at the desk, for just over ten minutes. Then Hophey came in with another man who carried a note pad. The other man sat in a nearby chair while Hophey, a stout man with little hair, sat behind his desk.

'Dear me,' said Hophey, shaking his head and speaking slowly. 'Can't you stay out of or away from trouble? Bit of a child problem: probation, Borstal, murder on New Tennon Street—and now this. This can put you away for a long time, son. A long time.'

Jamie knew it but hearing the copper say it jolted his inside a little.

'What, er, what exactly did Kilgrady have to do with this stolen jewellery?' Hophey wanted to know. 'You did work with him didn't you?'

Jamie shook his head. 'No, sir.'

'I don't suppose you had any idea that Kilgrady was related to a dangerous killer, did you?' said Hophey.

'The only killer I know of in Dion's family was his drunk dad,' said Jamie. 'And the only person he killed was 'issen.'

'Who's C. Chatterny?'

'Don't know. Never 'eard of 'im.'

'You must have heard of the "Marry-me" murderer,' said Hophey.

'I've read about 'im,' Jamie told him.

'That's who Chatterny is,' said Hophey. 'Real name: Ernest Keft. Dion Kilgrady's uncle. Now you know who Chatterny is, if you didn't already, you can tell me about your relationship with him.'

'I told you,' said Jamie. 'I never 'eard of any Chatterny.'

'You don't look too surprised to hear that Kilgrady was related to the "Marry-me" murderer,' said Hophey. 'Now look. An anonymous telephone call told us to go to Keft and Kilgrady's flat and we'd find the almighty Adam Clint there. This was the night Kilgrady was shot. Adam Clint is big stuff. What's he doing at Keft and Kilgrady's? And why did the anonymous caller phone us here at Tennon Street when there are police stations nearer that flat he could have tipped off? Now, you knew Chatterny. So let's hear it, lad.'

'I worked alone,' Jamie persisted. 'Honest.'

'All right!' Hophey demanded loudly: 'Give me a detailed picture of the biggest job you did!'

Jamie rubbed his red, sweaty forehead with his sleeve and stammered until he could think of something to put into a proper sentence. His mind was working slowly and it was showing him pictures of what had happened during the past few days since Thursday evening again. Jamie held on to the chair. He didn't have the will to search through his mixed-up mind to find something that would satisfy Hophey.

Hophey snapped words at him which he didn't grasp. It was so hot and dark in this room. 'What kind of weather is this for this time of year?' he asked himself. His mind pictured Julie, her big blue eyes watching him, sadly. It made his heart ache and for a minute he wished he could hold her to him like he had done on Sunday night. He knew how good it made him feel, yet the next minute he wondered if that was really what he wanted. He couldn't make up his mind.

He lifted his eyes and stared into Hophey's eyes. He forced tears into his own and said, in a hoarse voice, 'Don't —don't send me back, mister. I 'ave ter be wi' my girl. I need to be wi' 'er because—because I suppose I must love 'er. It—i—it's not that, it's ... Well we're so close, it's a new kind of friendship. An' it's just come to me that I could be inside ten years without 'er, and . . .'

'And you wouldn't like that, and I'm sorry for you,'

said Hophey. 'You should have thought about her when you stepped into a world where people kill people without blinking and sometimes get away with it. Clint's men are running around wild and free. And Miss Julie seems to be alone.'

'You wouldn't lerrem gerr'er would yer?' cried Jamie. 'Look, if you don't send me down I can tek her away ter London or somewhere.'

'Can't be done and you know that,' said Hophey. 'What is it? Sympathy you're after? That doesn't work here, lad. Maybe—maybe, I could put in a good word for you. If you told us all you know. *All* you know.'

Jamie gave up and spilled all, except for the parts about Kilgrady's gun, and finished his story with Cass bringing him to the police station and him identifying Kilgrady's killer's picture.

After this Jamie was taken to the cells and locked in one. He took his jacket off, unbuttoned his shirt and sat on the edge of the bunk.

He thought about what he was scared of. He'd be returning to Curris and Kellowyn Court, soon. Kellowyn Court: an unreal place where the walls, the fields, the trees and the sky were always colourless when he dreamt about it. He would be back there, probably for a longer time than the last. Then he realized that the last part of his sentence would be served in H.M. Prison and the thought knocked him back a bit. He lay back and lifted his legs up on to the bed and stared at the ceiling.

'Here you are in Bad Luck Street police station. Without a drink, without a fag, without Julie. "Anything you say may be taken down and used in evidence against you." Bad Luck Street. Tuh!'

Towards tea time his mother came with the solicitor, Lewis Main. Jamie told them what he had told the police.

He explained that trying to find a made-up story to palm the cops off with had been too much of a bloody effort for him and he had released the truth. He hadn't thought about seeing his solicitor first. 'I've put mesen away for a couple years. Ent Ah clever?'

Then Jamie turned his attention away from them and didn't take any special interest in what Mr. Main was telling him. It was done. The police had found him with the loot. Jamie couldn't see what could possibly be done about it.

He told his mother that he hadn't slept well the night before and he was now hot and tired. Dot looked worried and miserable. When they left he closed his eyes and after a while he dozed off to be roused soon after for some tea.

He fell asleep at just gone six o'clock and woke up in darkness at twenty to nine. His mind was playing with him. At first he thought he was at the Chapel of Rest looking at Dion Kilgrady lying in a coffin with candles burning at each end. It was all from a dream he'd just had. Jamie was imagining himself standing there looking in silence, with Julie hanging on to his right arm. Christ on the cross in the background wasn't Christ on the cross any more. It was Keft hanging from the gallows. Then, was that Julie hanging from the gallows? God no! Not that.

Julie! He wondered when he'd ever see her again after Kilgrady's inquest on Wednesday. He began to wish he hadn't told Hophey that he loved her. It must have sounded silly. He wished he could get away and become someone else.

In the back of his mind a whole world was in full swing twenty-four hours of the day. When he was awake he was only just aware of what was happening in his world, and at night he dreamt about it: all that was happening in his imaginary world of murderers, gangsters, guns, thieves, gossips, girls, dogs and cops. It was all like a film running in his mind, starring himself, Julie and Dion Kilgrady. Two heroes and a heroine. But there were too many enemies to fight and defeat. Keft, Clint, Hofton, Hophey, Cass, Wilf, Curris and the masters, and everyone at Knight and Drew's.

Kilgrady and Jamie fought, but never won. Rebels never win.

TEN

Jamie appeared in court and was tried for the stolen goods. Lewis Main defended him, for all the use it was. Jamie was finally told that he was to be sent back to Kellowyn Court for two years. Although he'd expected longer, it *did* set him back a bit when they told him.

His parents came to see him after. Wilf said nothing. He had thought his lad had been growing up. Now he was disappointed. Dot talked a lot about things working out better next time, with a bit of luck. And they went.

That night Jamie lay on his back on the bed, in darkness. Thinking about how they would laugh and make jokes on his return to Kellowyn. He'd have to face Curris. And the others. He'd have to stand to attention to the masters all over again; he'd have to roll his eyes away from those boys he had left there as enemies who would be laughing at him. Soon his friends like Norman, the Kellowyn 'queer', and Ellis, the Kellowyn 'cat' and the others would be leaving. When the last was gone he would do all he could to stay on his own. He'd concentrate on withdrawing his mind from the world. The lads wouldn't like it and maybe they would get him for it, but he didn't think he would care because for the first time in his life he felt he had the chance to become a real rebel. Looking back on the past few weeks he wasn't able to recognize himself as a rebel after all. At least not the type of rebel he had read about before. He had imagined himself as a rebel-hero and now he knew that if he was to become a rebel he would not become a hero. Like Don Gordon, Jamie would rebel alone. He'd keep himself cut off from the rest as well as he could until his release in two years' time and then when he was twenty he'd start his rebellion. He'd have no ties and would never become attached to anyone or any place. He'd let his hair grow unwashed and he wouldn't shave too often. All his clothes would be second hand and he'd wear them for years.

Suddenly Jamie remembered walking up New Tennon Street to the café with Bob and Lynn not long after leaving school. The time they had gone in and found Don Gordon sitting alone at a table. There had been a lot of teenagers about and music was belting out loud from the juke box. They found Don with tears running down his cheeks. His face had been straight, trying to hold them back. But there he was crying for all the world to see. When Jamie had asked him what was up with him he had replied, 'Looks silly, don't it? Big bloke cryin'. Lad like me bawlin' like a baby. Why does it look silly, though? Why shouldn't a man be allowed ter cry when 'e's sad, wi'out people laughin' at 'im an' sayin' 'e's girlish an' bleddy soft? Why shouldn't a bloke be allowed to laugh out as loud as he can when he's happy without people thinkin' 'e's a maniac an' wants lockin' up?' Maybe Jamie remembered this because during the past ten days there had been periods when he had wanted to cry and yet had been scared to except for the night he killed Keft, when he couldn't stop it. Now he was scared to cry, even alone in this cell. He wanted to cry, too, but somehow the tears wouldn't come. He wished they would. Never would he hide his emotions again. Whenever he would be unhappy he would cry; when he would be happy he would laugh. Don Gordon was right, Jamie thought, and maybe he always had been and was never wrong and had had nothing to do with planting the money stolen from Harpe's on him. Maybe Valerie *had* done it, as Don always said. How come he was on Don's side all of a sudden? He had failed to really understand Don before yet now, just because he was dead, he was feeling different about him. Jamie thought about that last fight. He could still see Don crumpled up against the wall like a crushed, stricken animal. He remembered that Don had never been the aggressive or athletic type. He lived in gentle moods of depression one minute and intense moods of deep depression the next. Jamie had been told that Don had been knocking about with one or two different girls for a while until he was seventeen when he bumped into this girl he'd known at school called Linda. Linda had been with her boy-friend. Don hadn't been seen with anyone since. Perhaps he was searching for another Linda. Seeking the same relationship in a girl as Jamie had found with Julie. Such a relationship is hard to find. Those who don't find it are lost.

'Why are you feelin' sorry for Don Gordon all of a sudden?' Jamie asked himself. Perhaps it was because in this cell he had been able to think more than he usually had, and he was able to righten things in his mind. He let his thoughts about Don fade from his mind, and tried not to think about Julie either. He must keep his mind off Julie at all costs to save him from feeling sorry for himself. But this was hard. Whatever he was trying to work out seemed, sooner or later, to be interrupted by Julie. Because of his trial and the mixed-up state of his mind, Jamie hadn't thought too much about Keft but he couldn't forget the warmth and comfort Julie had held out for him that Sunday night. In an irritable mood he wrote to her:

Dear Julie,

I suppose you'll know about it now. I'm back where I started. I hope you won't be too shocked about it all and me not writing before to tell you. It's spoilt everything. Everything we ever planned and talked about. By the same people as before. Oh yes, I've been in trouble with the law plenty of times before. But if they'd all left me alone I wouldn't be here. I'd be with you and that would be nice. Now it won't work. So don't hang about waiting for me because it won't be worth it. You keep away from the hidden streets and keep up with the writing. If I was you I'd move from Notts. Or at least go back to your parents.

I'll have to tell you now and get it done with but just in case you're wondering if I'll be back the answer is no, I won't. I suppose it's for the best really. I won't be seeing the old place again. I'll not be cycling to Castle Donnington again. I won't be visiting Breedon-on-the-Hill as I always used to do when I was a school kid and when I was cycling to see the castle ruins at Ashby-de-la-Zouch. I was never bothered about old Nottingham Castle, anyway.

The place won't exist from this day on as far as I'm concerned. Dion Kilgrady never existed. Wilf Howe is dead, Dorothy Howe is dead, Keft never lived, my Tennon Street gang were killed when they dropped the bomb on Tennon Street. Adam Clint never existed.

Yes, but the trouble is that Clint does exist. He's the big gangster and I know why he's in Nottingham now. He must have been planning to go on the con here. Know what I mean? I bet his big idea was to set up a ring of confidence tricksters like he has done in Soho. Plus pro's houses and drug centres. If Clint knew about Tennon Street I bet he would have made it his centre of operations in Nottingham because the Tennon St. people are stupid and dopey beyond belief, and dirt and mugs just waiting to be conned and gotten into trouble by people like the Clint mob, who want shooting because they wouldn't have lasted five minutes years ago. But here they are today—in our home city—putting the drug dealer who flogs dope from a room over a shop on Mansfield Road out of business and soon kids'll be fresh out of Ruffnall—junkies!

But do you remember the first night we met? That good night we had until I messed it up. I got left in our back garden all night and I woke up with me head feeling like a house brick had dropped on it. The garden was sort of spinning and there was this vile taste in me gob. Dion came round in the morning and got me on me feet. But if I worked at it I dare say I could drink and drink and drink and build me up a gut like my old man's.

I'll be going back to Kellowyn Court for sure. It ain't a very pleasant thing to look forward to. But I'm going to hold myself back. I'm not going to lash out at Curris and his strong-arm staff. Just going to keep myself turned in and silent until I get out. I'm going to stop myself rebelling against the bleeders with my fists. I'll just keep reading my books about rebels. Might even write a book about it, myself, one day. But I hope you come up with a bestseller soon, kidder. I hope you'll send me a copy when somebody publishes your book, and they will. I'll be able to hold it up for Kellowyn to see and I'll announce proudly that I used to know this little novelist.

But I'm a son of a bitch. I'm not exactly a desirable

person to know for anybody, never mind you. You go out and find yourself some right smashing boy-friend. I'm as second-rate as Kilgrady was. That's my conclusion.

Every best bit of luck to you. Dream happy.

> Best wishes,
> Goodnight,
> Jamie.

He had been irritable when he'd written this. And, perhaps, a little sorry for himself. When it was done and on its way to her he suddenly failed to see the point in writing such a letter. He'd just written a letter to the girl he thought he wanted, telling her to forget him. And now it was gone there was no way of stopping it reaching her. Now, because he was sorry, he made himself forget it. To write her another asking her to forget the first letter seemed too much of an effort.

The day after the trial Jamie was taken from his cell into a small dank room. There was only a desk and three chairs in there. It was a depressing little hole. The policeman who brought him down left him there alone. He sat there about twenty minutes before two plain-clothed men came in and closed the door behind them. Jamie felt nervous. He wondered what the hell all this could be about. One of the men was Davis, with his note book. The other man—a sullen-looking bloke—was a stranger to Jamie. He introduced himself as Superintendent Ian Bates. The policemen sat at the desk and Bates placed his folder in front of him.

'I bet you're wondering what all this is about, aren't you?' Bates smiled slightly.

Jamie gave a nod.

'I just want to ask you some questions,' said Bates. 'It's

probably nothing for you to worry over. I'd, er, I'd like to know where you were on the night of the twenty-fourth of November.'

'When?'

'Nine days ago.'

Jamie felt the colour rushing to his cheeks. His heart was paralysed for a few moments, then it started pounding away. Keft! They've identified Keft! They know! He held himself together, scared, but preparing himself for sharp questions he expected to be used as target for.

'Where were you?'

'Ah—Ah dunno,' Jamie blurted out. 'Derby, I think.'

'Derby, you think?' Bates raised his eyebrows. 'Jim, you were arrested on the twenty-sixth. If you were out on the Sunday night that must have been one of your last nights out. Can't you be sure? Do you often go over to Derby?'

'No! No, norroften.'

'Any particular reason for going that night?'

'Fancied a change.'

'You didn't go to visit anybody there you knew?'

'No. I just fancied a change.'

'Go with somebody, or were you alone?'

'Alone.'

'Bump into anybody you know by chance?'

'No. Look, what—I mean,' said Jamie. 'What's this all for? What's it all about?'

'Just answer the questions for now,' said Bates. 'If you were in Derby then you're clear.'

'Clear of *what*?'

The policeman answered quietly. 'Murder.'

Jamie felt shattered. It *was* Keft!

'Uh? I—I didn't kill anybody. Why me?'

'What time did you go to Derby?'

'Erm—arf-past seven.'

'When did you come home?'

'Closing time.'

'Where did you go?'

'Pictures.'

'Pictures? And you came out at closing time.'

'I, I came out o' the pictures arf way through the—the film an' wen' in a pub,' said Jamie.

'What film? What was it called?'

'I dunno. I, I—I missed the beginning.'

'What kind of a film was it, Jim? Cowboy? War? Musical? Horror? Sexy-exy? Murder . . . ?'

'Murder!'

'You didn't know what the film was called? What made you go into that particular cinema then? That's unusual, isn't it? When I go into a cinema it's because I fancy the film. I don't just go in like that.'

Jamie struggled for an answer.

'No. No, it wa' week before tharr I went ter the pictures. Er, I was in a pub all night.'

'Which pub was it?'

'The White Lion.'

'I'm just wondering about you, Jim,' said Bates, sitting back. 'I've told you you're being questioned in connection with a murder. But you haven't asked me who's been murdered.'

Jamie groaned inside himself. ''Oo as?'

'Ernest Keft. Your friend Charles Chatterny.'

'Him?' Jamie pretended to sound shocked.

'He was shot in the face,' said Bates.

'Aw, dear me! Well that's me off the suspect list for a start. I 'aven't gorra gun. Wouldn't know where to find one either.'

'Yes. Yes, well,' said Bates. 'You see, the murder weapon was left near the body. It was Dion Kilgrady's little Darker. And since Dion Kilgrady was himself murdered four days previous to this, we may presume that it wasn't *him* who killed Mr. Keft. That gun had been missing since Kilgrady's death. It was something that was very close to him. As he had a few nasty enemies about he always had this gun with him.'

'But he didn't the night 'e died.'

'Do you know that for certain?'

'If yer didn't find it i's obvious, i'n't it?' said Jamie.

'Do you know Bonnow Street?'

'Bonnow Street?' Jamie looked down and spoke out loud to himself. 'Bonnow, Bonnow. Let's see. Bonnow.' He looked up. 'Near cut, en' it?'

'You know the place.'

'If it's near the cut I think I know which road you mean,' said Jamie.

'You're sure it was Derby you were at and not anywhere around Bonnow Street?'

'Dead sure, I am.'

'What time did you get home from Derby?'

'I dunno. 'Bout twen'y ter twelve, maybe.'

'Go to bed then?'

'Yeh.'

'Work next morning?'

'Yeh . . .' Jamie remembered he'd been at Julie's and the police could check up at Knight's to see whether he had gone in or not that day. 'No. I, I overslept. So I di'n't bother goin' in. I spent the day at a friend's 'ouse.'

'Miss Dean's flat,' said Bates.

'What made you say that?' asked Jamie.

'Come on, laddie. These lies are getting you nowhere.'

Jamie thought he was going to faint. 'Uh?'

'*Lies*. Everything.' Bates leaned his elbows back on the desk. 'How about coughing up the truth? Did you kill Keft?'

'How . . . how . . . how could I?' Jamie tried to cough a lump out of his throat.

'Didn't you run off with Kilgrady's gun the night he was killed?' questioned Bates. 'Didn't you shoot Keft? Was it only an accident? Or self-defence? He was shooting at you, wasn't he? You shot back. You killed him.'

'I did not. You've gorra believe what I'm sayin'. I didn't. Why are you sayin' all that? I don't understand why you should say that.'

'You weren't at Derby that night, laddie,' said Bates. 'You were at Bonnow Street. There are witnesses.'

That set Jamie back.

'You didn't go home either. You spent the night at 14 J Lincoln Hill. You arrived there shouting and banging. The next day a young lady—Miss Dean—telephoned your father at his work and told him you'd be staying at her parents' for a few days. You hadn't been home after going out on Sunday evening.'

'Who . . . told you? Julie?'

'Your father. We also questioned Miss Dean.'

Jamie felt miserable. 'She's told 'em. I know what 'e means when 'e says 'e questioned 'er, the son of a bitch. And she's told 'em.'

'You were seen on Bonnow Street at close to nine o'clock, Sunday, November twenty-fourth,' said Bates.

Jamie thought back to nine days ago. The only person who had seen him at Bonnow Street was his old friend Bob Denham. Had Bob gone and done this to him?'

'Not . . . not Bobby Denham?'

' "Members of the public in that vicinity between nine and ten on that night please contact the police",' said Bates. 'Young Mr. Denham stepped up, and he happened to drop your name. The day we picked you up we also picked up a man known as "Fence" Wesson. We arrested him at your Wollaton house. When he heard of the unidentified body being found in the scrap-yard he told us Keft expected to meet you there.

'So, Jim—you didn't agree on the price Keft had let the loot go at. Did you fight? Keft tried to kill you, but you killed him . . .'

'Why don't you believe me?' moaned Jamie.

'You dropped the gun. You were shaken. You were shocked at what you'd done. You ran off and found your way to Lincoln Hill. Julie wasn't home, and a man came out of one of the rooms to see what all the noise you were making was about. You rang Julie and she came to the rescue. It was you who killed Keft. We have your fingerprints on the gun. Now, are you ready to tell us how it happened?'

Jamie's desperate hopes and determination collapsed. He looked down at his hands on his lap. 'Uh. I'd . . . I'd be dead mesen if I 'adn't tripped over . . . an' killed 'im.'

Jamie's fingerprints were taken again and matched with those on the gun. He was charged with murder in the afternoon. Back in his cell he felt as if he had fallen and would never be able to get up again. Later in the day his mother came. She was very distressed. The police had notified her that her son was on a murder charge. She had with her a letter for Jamie. He read it.

14 J Lincoln Hill,
Nottingham.
December 2nd

Dear Jamie,

I'm very sorry you don't want to see me again. I wish things had been different, too. It makes me very unhappy to think you're going away, and I feel very hurt that you want me to wipe you out of my mind. How can I after all that's happened?

The police know what you did to that man. I tried to side-step them but their questions were so sharp and persistent that they caught me out. I tried to lie for you, honest to God I did. But in the end I had to tell them. I'm sorry. I bet you hate me now. I don't blame you.

It's hard to write to you. It's hard to find the words to say, so I'd better not try. I'd better leave it at that.

I'm sorry.

Love from,
Julie.

Jamie screwed the paper in his hands and cried.

'Jamie, luv,' cried Dot, leaning forward to touch him. But he didn't even see her. He was taken back to his cell and calmed by a police officer.

ELEVEN

Christmas was a week away. Jamie was going through another long restless night in his cell. He lay on his back staring up at the darkness. And one minute he turned this way and the next he turned that way. There was no sleep in his eyes. He knew he would remain awake for hours and then fall into a heavy comfortable sleep five minutes before getting-up time. He wished he could get Julie out of his mind. It was her keeping him awake. He'd been thinking about her all afternoon. Her face stuck in his mind and in the little world at the back of his mind. Jamie had never really got to loving her. He hadn't paid enough attention to her. He wished he had taken her into her bedroom and undressed her and made love to her. He wished he had really loved her instead of running around playing Mad Dog Coll with Keft and Kilgrady. He wished she was there for him now. And he bit his tongue. He cried and closed his eyes, hoping that when he opened them he would find that special girl sitting on the edge of his bed unbuttoning her blouse. For a few seconds, when he did open them, he saw a figure in the darkness of just that. But then it disappeared. The only girl who had wanted him in the right way. If only he could get up now and write her a letter pleading for her to wait for him. He had it all written out in his mind so that when daylight came in a few hours' time he would be able to scribble it down with a dip-pen.

'What a son of a Tennon Street whore I am,' he spoke out quietly. He remembered he had used Julie and the word 'love' while Hophey had been questioning him and he wondered if the Tennon Street cops were laughing at him because they knew what type of person he was. Maybe his love for her had just been an excuse. Trying to show Tennon Street what a confused teenager he was.

Each minute crept by like an hour and Jamie's eyes never closed. They stared into the darkness. In the world at the back of his mind he was driving a green bus. He was driving it along Housenal Street. Driving fast and straight ahead. The sign reading 'New Tennon Street' appeared. Jamie tried turning the steering wheel. It was stiff. With all his strength he twisted the steering wheel to the left and swung the vehicle off Housenal Street on to New Tennon. The bus raced up New Tennon Street going faster and faster. Jamie couldn't stop it. He fought with the wheel again to turn it right, on to Tennon Street. He managed, and down it went racing towards Lower Tennon Street and Rain Street. A motor cycle swerved out and roared past him at terrific speed, disappearing into the distance out of sight. 'The bleddy fool! What's he tryin' to do—kill 'issen?' he exclaimed. He laughed like a madman as Tennon Street filth leaped out of his way. As the bus neared Husingden Street, Julie came running out, screaming. Behind her, with a piece of material torn from her dress in his hands, ran a rough-looking youth. He had a couple of days' growth on his chin, black hair hanging over his eyes and was very drunk. He was dressed in a suit that had once been expensive but was now dirty and ragged. This dangerous pursuer was Dion Kilgrady, snarling and spitting. He had been chasing Julie down a dark, lonely, narrow street. Julie was trying to escape from what looked like a creation of the devil. She was trying to escape from the supernatural, the unclean. Jamie tried to slow the bus down to make it easy for her to jump on. But the bus increased its speed instead. Julie leapt for her life, caught the rail and landed on the platform. The bus sped on. Together Jamie and Julie had escaped. In one of those green buses that never go up Tennon Street. In reality Jamie couldn't escape from the world, he could only daydream.

Poor Julie. She was the only person he had ever cared for and the only person who had ever really cared for him. She had even stayed with him and helped and comforted him when he had told her that he had killed a man. She'd stood by him. Who else would have done that? He cried silently. There were a lot of tears for him to cry and when he was drained of all his tears he wished he could go on and on crying.

'Bleddy 'ell,' he whimpered.

He rolled over.